# Barabbas

## By PÄR LAGERKVIST

*Translated by* ALAN BLAIR

*With a preface by* LUCIEN MAURY

*and a letter by* ANDRÉ GIDE

D0051674

**VINTAGE BOOKS**

A DIVISION OF RANDOM HOUSE

*New York*

VINTAGE BOOKS

*are published by Alfred A. Knopf, Inc.*

*and Random House, Inc.*

*Library of Congress Catalog Card Number: 55–5728*

Manufactured in the United States of America

# Preface

In a body of literature which has been for the most part preoccupied with national background, with painting the manners of Stockholm and of the Swedish countryside, and — apart from its exploitation of a rich lyric strain — with folklore and epic fantasy, Pär Lagerkvist, since his early "Expressionist" days, has stood as representative of an intellectualism which, like himself, has remained somewhat remote and dignified, somewhat unresponsive to the noisy methods of modern publicity.

In the world of Swedish and Scandinavian letters, Lagerkvist occupies, as poet and thinker, a position of eminence which has long been recognized by his compatriots and by the educated public in the countries which adjoin his own. To paint the portrait of this remarkable man, whose work takes rank with the most significant productions of contemporary Scandinavia, is as tempting as it would be difficult.

Except for a few short stories, and one piece of dramatic narrative, *The Dwarf,* which was highly praised by our literary critics, the French public knows next to nothing of his writings.

Before saying anything else, it is well to draw attention to characteristics which are pre-eminent in the whole body of his work — to a nobility of tone and of style, to an unquestioning devotion to independence of mind, to an unequivocal sense of vocation which, for half a century, has assured for him a deserved reputation as one of the "advance guard."

There is scarcely a single æsthetic problem in the realm of literature which Lagerkvist has not striven to define and resolve — not only theoretically, but in the practice of his art — whether in the theatre, the short story, or works of meditation, and verse. He has passed through many stages, from his early concern with the art of the theatre at a time when Copeau and Gordon Craig were making their first experiments, a concern which led to conclusions as daring and as relevant now as they ever were, to those hybrid productions, sometimes published simultaneously in the form of narratives or plays — *The Man Who Lived Again; The Dwarf; The Man Without a Soul; The Hangman; Victory in Darkness; The Philoso-*

*pher's Stone.* He has travelled far from the *Tales of Cruelty* — which have only a title in common with the stories of Villiers de l'Isle-Adam — or the deeply moving short pieces marked by an eloquent simplicity which the French writer Louis Philippe would not have disowned; from those chapters of autobiography which reveal a meditative childhood already haunted by strange presentiments, and a curious hankering after death, to those essays and poems marked by a thrilling tenseness of unease, and filled with metaphysical ardour. It has been a far cry with him from anguish to serenity, to that interior joy which triumphs over all despair; from early revolt to an acceptance which has never been mere resignation, though often it is not far removed from a mood of burning adoration, from a religious sense at one with reason, from faith in the existence of a principle to be found at the source of all our human destiny. Many phases mark his pilgrimage, and the victories he has won are numerous in battles joined on the fields of ethics and æsthetics, in the perpetual struggle to attain to those realms of thought where the spirit can find its ultimate well-being.

Had Pär Lagerkvist written in a language more easily accessible to Western readers, he would undoubtedly have been acclaimed as one of the leaders of our time, as one of those few, those necessary, men who can hold aloft a light to guide our footsteps through the obsessive darkness of our world.

The little work here offered in translation proves abundantly that he has never lost touch with the tragedy of the contemporary mind, that, in spite of his philosophy, he is familiar with the devastating terrors of our problems, and has been brought face to face with the insoluble problem of Man's predicament, with the horror of that blindness in which we are compelled to face the problem of the universe and of ourselves.

In this enigmatic and unforgettable *Barabbas*, with its sense of spiritual torment, its deep stirrings of faith, its sure response to the movements of the human mind, is expressed the riddle of Man and his destiny, the contrasted aspects of his fundamental drama, and the cry of humanity in its death throes, bequeathing its spirit to the night.

In this, his latest work, we see the final development of an art which has reached the limits of elliptic suggestion, of austerity, and of a form that has been pared down to essentials.

*Barabbas* is the last phase in a process of thought

which has moved beyond mere literature, of an art which, with its admirable sobriety, embodies the emotional climate of our times.

Lucien Maury

M<small>Y</small> D<small>EAR</small> L<small>UCIEN</small> M<small>AURY</small>:

Pär Lagerkvist's *Barabbas* is, beyond all possibility of doubt, a remarkable book. I am deeply grateful to you for giving me an early opportunity to read it, as you did in the case of the same author's *The Dwarf* which received, last year, so enthusiastic a welcome from critics and public alike.

When you brought me the translation of *Barabbas,* you spoke of it in such a way as to make me feel the liveliest desire to read it. But I had no idea then how deeply it would interest me. I was, as it so happened, marvellously (I dare not say, providentially) prepared for the experience of its perusal owing to the fact that I had been buried, for the past month, in a study of *l'Histoire des Origines du Christianisme.* Renan had, in masterly fashion, made it possible for me to realize with what intelligent precision Pär

Lagerkvist has shown the mysterious springs of an emerging conscience secretly tormented by the problem of Christ at a time when the Christian doctrine was still in the process of formation, when the dogma of the Resurrection still depended on the uncertain evidence of a few credulous witnesses who had not yet bridged the gap between superstition and faith.

From what you told me then, my dear Maury, I derived a very imperfect idea of the extent to which the adventure of Barabbas was involved in the story of Our Lord's crucifixion, of the degree to which the troubled movements of the robber's mind were bound up with what he had seen, or thought he had seen, at Golgotha, and with the various rumours which followed hard upon the Divine Tragedy — an event upon which the destiny of well-nigh the whole of humanity was, eventually, to hang.

It is the measure of Lagerkvist's success that he has managed so admirably to maintain his balance on a tightrope which stretches across the dark abyss that lies between the world of reality and the world of faith. The closing sentence of the book remains (no doubt deliberately) ambiguous: "When he felt death approaching, that which he had always been so afraid of, he said out into the darkness, as though he were speaking to it: — To thee I deliver up my soul." That "as though" leaves me wondering whether, without realizing it, he was, in fact, addressing Christ, whether the Galilean did not "get him" at the end. Vicisti Galileus, as Julian the Apostate said.

I have your word for it, dear Maury, that this ambiguity exists also in the original text. The Swedish language has given us, and is still giving, works of such outstanding value, that knowledge of it will soon form part of the equipment of any man calling himself well-educated. We need to be in the position to appreciate the important part likely to be played by Sweden in the Concert of Europe.

ANDRÉ GIDE

# BARABBAS

EVERYONE knows how they hung there on the crosses, and who they were that stood gathered around him: Mary his mother and Mary Magdalene, Veronica, Simon of Cyrene, who carried the cross, and Joseph of Arimathea, who shrouded him. But a little further down the slope, rather to one side, a man was standing with his eyes riveted on the dying man in the middle, watching his death-throes from the first moment to the last. His name was Barabbas. This book is about him.

He was about thirty, powerfully built, with a sallow complexion, a reddish beard and black hair. His eyebrows also were black, his eyes too deep-set, as though they wanted to hide. Under one of them he had a deep scar that was lost to sight in his beard. But a man's appearance is of little consequence.

He had followed the mob through the streets all

the way from the governor's palace, but at a distance, somewhat behind the others. When the exhausted rabbi had collapsed beneath his cross, he had stopped and stood still for a while to avoid catching up with the cross, and then they had got hold of that man Simon and forced him to carry it instead. There were not many men in the crowd, except the Roman soldiers of course; they were mostly women following the condemned man and a flock of urchins who were always there when anyone was led out along their street to be crucified — it made a change for them. But they soon tired and went back to their games, pausing a moment to glance at the man with the long scar down his cheek who was walking behind the others.

Now he was standing up here on the gallows-hill looking at the man on the middle cross, unable to tear his eyes away. Actually he had not wanted to come up here at all, for everything was unclean, full of contagion; if a man set foot in this potent and accursed place part of him would surely remain, and he could be forced back there, never to leave it again. Skulls and bones lay scattered about everywhere, together with fallen, half-mouldering crosses, no longer of any use but left to lie there all the same, because no one would touch anything. Why was he standing here? He did not know this man, had nothing to do with him. What was he doing at Golgotha, he who had been released?

The crucified man's head hung down and he was breathing heavily; it would not be long now. There was nothing vigorous about the fellow. His body was lean and spindly, the arms slender as though they had never been put to any use. A queer man. The beard was sparse and the chest quite hairless, like a boy's. He did not like him.

From the first moment Barabbas had seen him in the courtyard of the palace, he had felt there was something odd about him. What it was he could not say; it was just something he felt. He didn't remember ever having seen anyone like him before. Though it must have been because he came straight from the dungeon and his eyes were still unused to the glare. That is why at first glance the man seemed to be surrounded by a dazzling light. Soon afterwards the light vanished, of course, and his sight grew normal again and took in other things besides the figure standing out there alone in the courtyard. But he still thought there was something very strange about him and that he was not like anyone else. It seemed quite

5

incredible that he was a prisoner and had been condemned to death, just as he himself had been. He could not grasp it. Not that it concerned him — but how could they pass a sentence like that? It was obvious he was innocent.

Then the man had been led out to be crucified — and he himself had been unshackled and told he was free. It was none of his doing. It was their business. They were quite at liberty to choose whomever they liked, and it just turned out that way. They had both been sentenced to death, but one of them was to be released. He was amazed himself at their choice. As they were freeing him from his chains, he had seen the other man between the soldiers disappear through the archway, with the cross already on his back.

He had remained standing, looking out through the empty arch. Then the guard had given him a push and bellowed at him: — What are you standing there gaping for, get out of here, you're free! And he had awakened and gone out through the same archway, and when he saw the other dragging his cross down the street he had followed behind him. Why, he did not know. Nor why he had stood here hour after hour watching the crucifixion and the long death agony, though it was nothing whatever to do with him.

Those standing around the cross up there surely need not have been here? Not unless they had wanted to. Nothing was forcing them to come along and defile themselves with uncleanness. But they were no doubt relations and close friends. Odd that they didn't seem to mind being made unclean.

That woman must be his mother. Though she was not like him. But who could be like him? She looked like a peasant woman, stern and morose, and she kept wiping the back of her hand across her mouth and nose, which was running because she was on the brink of tears. But she did not cry. She did not grieve in the same way as the others, nor did she look at him in the same way as they did. So it was evidently his mother. She probably felt far more sorry for him than they did, but even so she seemed to reproach him for hanging there, for having let himself be crucified. He must have done something to let himself in for it, however pure and innocent he was, and she just could not approve of it. She knew he was innocent because she was his mother. Whatever he had done she would have thought so.

He himself had no mother. And no father either, for that matter; he had never even heard one mentioned. And he had no relatives, as far as he knew. So if he had been the one to be crucified there would not have been many tears shed. Not like this. They were beating their breasts and carrying on as though they had never known the like of such grief, and there was an awful weeping and wailing the whole time.

He knew the one on the right-hand cross quite well. If by any chance the fellow saw him standing down here, he probably thought it was because of him, in order to see him suffer well and truly. He wasn't, he was not here because of that at all. But he had nothing against seeing him crucified. If anyone deserved to die, it was that scoundrel. Though not because of what he had been sentenced for, but because of something quite different.

But why was he looking at him and not at the one in the middle, who was hanging there in his stead? It was because of him he had come. This man had forced him up here, he had a strange power over him. Power? If anyone looked powerless, he did. Surely no one could look more wretched hanging on a cross. The other two didn't look a bit like that and didn't seem to be suffering as much as he was. They obviously had more strength left. He hadn't even the strength to hold his head up; it had flopped right down.

Now he did raise it a bit, all the same; the lean, hairless chest heaved with panting, and his tongue licked his parched lips. He groaned something about being thirsty. The soldiers who were sprawled over a game of dice a little further down the slope, bored because the men hanging there took so long to die, did not hear. But one of the relatives went down and told them. A soldier got up reluctantly and dipped a sponge in a pitcher, passing it up to him on a stick, but when he tasted the fusty, tainted liquid offered him he did not want it. The wretch just stood there grinning, and when he rejoined his companions they all lay grinning at what had happened. The bastards!

The relatives or whoever they were looked despairingly up at the crucified man, who was panting and panting; it was clear that he would soon give up the ghost. And just as well if the end came soon, Barabbas thought, so that the poor man would not have to suffer any more. If only the end would come! As soon as the end came he would hurry away and never think of this again. . . .

But all at once the whole hill grew dark, as though

9

the light had gone out of the sun; it was almost pitch-dark, and in the darkness above, the crucified man cried out in a loud voice:

— My God, my God, why hast thou forsaken me?

It sounded horrible. Whatever did he mean? And why had it grown dark? It was the middle of the day. It was quite unaccountable. The three crosses were just faintly visible up there. It looked weird. Something terrible was surely going to happen. The soldiers had leapt to their feet and grabbed their weapons; whatever happened they always rushed for their weapons. They stood there around the crosses with their lances, and he heard them whispering together in alarm. Now they were frightened! Now they were not grinning any longer! They were superstitious, of course.

He was afraid himself. And glad when it began to get light and everything became a little more normal. It got light slowly, as it does at dawn. The daylight spread across the hill and the olive trees around about, and the birds that had been silent started twittering again. It was just like dawn.

The relatives up there were standing so still. There was no longer any sound of weeping and lamentation from them. They just stood looking up at the man on the cross; even the soldiers did so. Everything had grown so still.

Now he could go whenever he liked. For it was all over now, and the sun shone again and everything was just as usual. It had only been dark for a while because the man had died.

Yes, he would go now. Of course he would. He had nothing to stay for, not now that he, that other one, was dead. There was no longer any reason. They took him down from the cross, he saw before he went. The two men wrapped him in a clean linen cloth, he noticed. The body was quite white and they handled it so carefully, as if they were afraid they might hurt it, however slightly, or cause it pain of any kind. They behaved so strangely. After all, he was crucified and everything. They were queer people, to be sure. But the mother stood with dry eyes looking at what had been her son, and the rough, dark-complexioned face seemed unable to express her sorrow, only the fact that she could not grasp what had happened and would never be able to forgive it. He understood her better.

As the sorry procession moved past some little distance from him, the men carrying the shrouded body and the women walking behind, one of the women

**11**

whispered to the mother — pointing to Barabbas. She stopped short and gave him such a helpless and reproachful look that he knew he could never forget it. They went on down towards the Golgotha road and then turned off to the left.

He followed far enough behind for them not to notice him. In a garden a short distance away they laid the dead man in a tomb that was hewn out of the rock. And when they had prayed by the tomb they rolled a large stone in front of the entrance and went away.

He walked up to the tomb and stood there for a while. But he did not pray, for he was an evil-doer and his prayer would not have been accepted, especially as his crime was not expiated. Besides, he did not know the dead man. He stood there for a moment, all the same.

Then he too went in towards Jerusalem.

INSIDE the Gate of David and a little way along the street he met the girl with the hare-lip. She was hugging the walls of the houses and pretended not to see him, but he noticed that she had done so and that she had not expected to see him again. Perhaps she thought he had been crucified.

He walked along behind her and then caught up with her, and so it was they met. It need not have happened. He need not have spoken to her, and was himself surprised that he had done so. She, too, from what he could make out. She glanced at him shyly when she had to.

They did not speak of what was in their minds; he merely asked her where she was going and if she had heard anything from Gilgal. She answered no more than was necessary and slurred her words as usual, so that it was hard to catch what she said. She was not going anywhere, and when he asked where she lived she made no reply. He saw that her skirt hung in tatters around the hem and that her broad, dirty feet were bare. Their conversation lapsed and they walked on beside each other without a word.

From an open doorway like a black hole came the sound of loud voices, and, just as they passed, a large fat woman came rushing out and shouted at Barabbas. She was tipsy and waved her fat arms with excitement and joy at seeing him, wanting him to come in without further ado. He hesitated and also seemed rather embarrassed by the presence of his strange companion, but she merely tugged at him and shoved them both inside. He was greeted with shouts by two men and three women whom he could not see at first, until his eyes had got used to the semi-darkness. They eagerly made room for him at the table, pouring out wine for him and all talking at once about his having been let out of prison and being discharged and how damned lucky he was that the other one had been crucified in his place. They overflowed with wine and desire to share his good fortune, touching him to transfer it to themselves, and one of the women stuck her hand in under his body garment and touched his hairy chest, which made the fat woman roar with laughter.

Barabbas drank with them but said little. He sat for the most part gazing in front of him with the dark brown eyes that were too deep-set, as though they wanted to hide. They thought he was a little queer. Though of course he was like that sometimes.

The women poured out more wine for him. He went on drinking and let them talk, joining very little in the conversation himself.

At last they began asking what was the matter with him, why he was like that. But the large fat woman put her arm around his neck and said that it wasn't any wonder he seemed a bit queer after lying chained up in a dungeon for so long, very nearly dead; if a man is sentenced to death, then he's dead, and if he's let out and reprieved he's still dead, because that's what he has been and he's only risen again from the dead, and that's not the same as living and being like the rest of us. And when they grinned at what she said, she lost her temper and said she would throw them all out except Barabbas and the girl with the hare-lip whom she knew nothing about but who looked good-natured, she thought, though a bit simple. The two men nearly split their sides laughing at a woman who talked to them like that, but then they quieted down and began a whispered conversation with Barabbas, saying that they were going up into the mountains again tonight as soon as it was dark; they had only been down here to sacrifice a kid they had brought. It had not been accepted, so they had sold it and sacrificed two stainless doves instead. Then, having some money to spare, they had spent it on a good time at this fat woman's. They wondered when he would be back up there again and told him where their den was now. Barabbas nodded in understanding but made no answer.

One of the women had begun talking about the man who had been crucified in Barabbas's place. She had seen him once, though only as he was walking past, and people had said that he was a man learned in the scriptures who went about prophesying and performing miracles. There was no harm in that and there were many who did it, so of course it must have been something else he was crucified for. He was a skinny fellow, that was all she remembered. Another woman said that she had never seen him but had heard he was supposed to have said that the temple would collapse and Jerusalem be destroyed by an earthquake and then both heaven and earth would be consumed by fire. It sounded crazy, and it was not surprising that he had been crucified because of it.

But the third said that he had mixed mostly with the poor and used to promise them that they would enter the kingdom of God; even the harlots, and that greatly amused them all, though they thought it was very nice, provided it were true.

Barabbas listened to them and no longer seemed to be so far away, though he never so much as smiled. He gave a start when the fat woman again put her arm around his neck and said that she didn't care a fig who that other man was, he was dead now anyway. It was he who had been crucified and not Barabbas, and that was the main thing.

The girl with the hare-lip had at first sat huddled up, to all appearances inattentive. She had then listened tensely to the description of that other man, and now acted rather strangely. Getting up, she stared at her companion from the street with an expression of horror in her pale, emaciated face, and exclaimed in her queer, snuffling voice:

— Barabbas!

It was nothing remarkable in itself; she had only called him by his name, but they looked at her in amazement, unable to grasp what she meant by crying out like that. Barabbas too seemed strange, and his eyes kept shifting about as they did sometimes when he wanted to avoid looking at anyone. Why it was, they didn't understand; anyway, it didn't matter, and it was best not to take any notice. For whatever one might say about Barabbas's being a good comrade and all that, he was a bit odd — one never really knew where one was with him.

She huddled up again on her bit of matting over on the earthen floor, but still went on looking at him with her burning eyes.

The fat woman went and got food for Barabbas. It occurred to her he must be starving; those dirty swine probably gave their prisoners nothing to eat. She set bread and salt and a piece of dried mutton in front of him. He ate but little, soon handing what was left across to the girl with the hare-lip, as though he were already satisfied. She threw herself on it and devoured it like an animal, then rushed out of the house; quite suddenly she was not there.

They ventured to ask what sort of woman she was, but of course got no answer. That was typical of him. He was always like that, secretive about his own affairs.

— What sort of miracles did he perform, that preacher, he said, turning to the women, and what did he preach about, for that matter?

18

They said that he healed the sick and drove out evil spirits; he was supposed to have raised people from the dead too, but nobody knew if it was true; it couldn't be, of course. What he preached about, they had no idea. But one of them had heard a story he was supposed to have told about someone who arranged a big feast, a wedding or something, but no guests arrived, so they had to go out into the streets and invite just anybody, and all they could get were beggars and poor starving wretches who scarcely had a rag to their backs, and then the great lord got angry, or at any rate he said that it didn't matter — no, she couldn't remember properly how it was. Barabbas seemed to be listening intently the whole time, as though they had related something quite extraordinary. And when one of the women said that he must have been one of those who believed themselves to be the Messiah, he stroked his great red beard and sat lost in thought. — The Messiah? . . . No, he wasn't the Messiah, he mumbled to himself.

— No, of course he couldn't be, said one of the men, for then they would never have been able to crucify him, then those bastards themselves would have been struck to the ground. Didn't she know what a Messiah was?

**19**

— No, of course! In that case he would have come down from the cross and slain the lot of them.

— A Messiah who lets himself be crucified! Did you ever hear the like!

Barabbas remained sitting with his beard in his big hand, looking down at the earthen floor. — No, he wasn't the Messiah. . . .

— Oh, drink up now, Barabbas, and don't sit there muttering, said one of his confederates, poking him in the ribs. It was strange his daring to do so, but he did. And Barabbas actually took a draught from the earthenware beaker, putting it down again abstractedly. The women quickly filled it up again and got him to swallow another draught. The wine must have had some effect, but his thoughts still seemed to be elsewhere. The man gave him another prod with his elbow.

— Come now, have a drink and cheer up! Aren't you glad you're out of it and sitting here enjoying yourself among friends instead of hanging rotting on a cross? Isn't this better, eh? Aren't you having a good time here, eh? Think of that, Barabbas. You've saved your bacon, you're alive. You're *alive*, Barabbas!

— Yes. Yes, of course, he said. Of course . . .

In this way they gradually got him to stop staring

into space like that and to become more normal. They sat drinking and talking for a while about one thing and another, and there was nothing queer about him any longer, they thought.

But in the middle of discussing this and that he asked a strange question. He asked them what they thought about the darkness today, when the light had gone out of the sun for a time.

— Darkness? What darkness? They looked at him in astonishment. It hadn't been dark, had it? When?

— About the sixth hour?

— Pshaw . . . What rubbish! No one had seen anything like that.

He looked incredulously from one to the other, quite bewildered. They all assured him they had not noticed any darkness, nor had anyone else in the whole of Jerusalem. Had he really thought it got dark? In the middle of the day? How very peculiar! But if he really had thought so, then it must be because there was something wrong with his eyes after lying shut up in the dungeon for so long. Yes, that's probably what it was. The fat woman said that of course it must be due to that, to the fact that his eyes had not got used to the light, that he had been blinded by the light for a while. And no wonder, either.

He looked at them doubtfully, and then appeared relieved in some way. He straightened himself a little and reached out his hand for the beaker — took a deep draught out of it. And then, instead of putting it back on the table, kept it in his hand and held it out for more. It was given to him instantly; they all drank, and he was clearly beginning to relish the wine in quite a different way. He drank as he normally did when it was offered and they could see it put him in a better mood. He did not grow especially communicative, but he did tell them something about what it had been like in prison. Yes, he'd had a hell of a time, of course, no wonder he was a bit light-headed. But to think he had got out, eh! It wasn't so easy once they got their claws into you. What luck, eh! First that he had been there waiting to be crucified just at the Passover, when they usually release somebody. And then that it should have been he, of all people! What infernal good luck! He thought so too, and when they pushed him and thumped him on the back and sprawled over him with their heated breath he smiled and drank with them, one after the other. He thawed as the wine rose to his head, and became more and more lively, loosening his body garment because of the heat, and lying down and making himself comfortable like the others. He was obviously enjoying himself. He even put his arm around the woman nearest him and pulled her towards him. She laughed and hung around his neck. But the fat woman took him from her and said that now her darling was really himself again, now he was as he should be and quite well again after that dreadful prison. And never again was he to go imagining things about any silly darkness, nonono, tuttuttut . . . She pulled him to her and made little caressing noises all over his face with her pouted lips, fondling the back of his neck with her fat fingers and playing with his red beard. They were all pleased at the change in him and that he was more himself, more like he could be sometimes when he was in a good mood. And now they all let themselves go whole-heartedly. They drank and gabbled and agreed about everything and found they were having a good time together, lying there inflaming themselves with the wine and with each other. The men, who had not tasted wine or seen a woman for several months, made up for it now. Soon they would be going back to their mountains; they hadn't much time left. . . . Now they must really celebrate being in Jerusalem, and celebrate Barabbas's release! They got drunk on the strong, sour wine and amused themselves with all the women except the fat one, pulling them in one after the other behind a curtain further inside and coming back flushed and panting to resume their drinking and noise. They did everything thoroughly, as was their wont.

They continued in this way until it began to grow dark. Then the two men got up and said it was time they were going. Throwing their goat-skins over their shoulders and hiding their weapons under them, they said good-bye and crept out into the street, where it was already nearly dark. Soon afterwards the three women went and lay down behind the curtain, tipsy and utterly exhausted, and fell fast asleep. When the fat woman and Barabbas were thus left alone, she asked if he didn't think it was about time they too enjoyed themselves together, if he wasn't in need of it after having been treated so badly. She for her part greatly fancied one who had languished so long in prison and so nearly been crucified. She took him up onto the roof, where she had a little arbour made of palm leaves for the hot time of the year. They lay down and she fondled him a little and he grew quite wild, wallowing in her fat body as though he never wanted to leave it. Half the night passed by without their being conscious of anything round them.

When at last they were quite spent she turned over on her side and fell asleep at once. He lay awake beside her sweaty body, looking up at the roof of the arbour. He thought of the man on the middle cross and of what had happened up there on the gallows-hill. Then he began to wonder about that darkness, and whether it had really happened. Could it be as they said, merely something he had imagined? Or perhaps it was just something up there at Golgotha, as they had noticed nothing here in the city? Up there anyway it had been dark; the soldiers had been scared, and one thing and another — or had he imagined that too? Had he just imagined the whole thing? No, he could not work it out, didn't know what to make of it. . . .

Barabbas thought of him again, the man on the cross. He lay with his eyes open, unable to sleep, feeling the woman's fleshy body against him. Through the dry leaves on the roof he could see up into the sky — it must be the sky, although no stars were to be seen. Nothing but the darkness.

For now it was dark both at Golgotha and everywhere else.

Next day Barabbas walked about the city and met many whom he knew, both friend and foe. Most of them seemed surprised to see him, and one or two started as though they had seen a ghost. It gave him a nasty feeling. Didn't they know he had been released? When would they realize it — that it was not he who had been crucified?

The sun beat down, and it was extraordinary how hard it was to accustom his eyes properly to the glare. Perhaps something really had gone wrong with them during his time in prison? He preferred to keep in the shade, anyway. As he passed the colonnade in the street leading up to the temple he went in and sat under the arches to rest his eyes for a while. It felt good.

One or two men were already sitting huddled along the wall. They were talking in an undertone and seemed to resent his arrival, looking sideways at him and lowering their voices still more. He caught a word here and there but could make no sense of it; what of it anyway, he didn't care what secret dealings they had. One of them was a man of about his own age and with a red beard too; the hair, also red, was long and tousled and joined the beard. The eyes were blue, which gave a curious, simple appearance, and the face was large and fleshy. Everything about him was large. He was a real rough diamond, an artisan, judging from his hands and clothes. It didn't matter to Barabbas who he was or what he looked like, but he was the kind of man one couldn't help noticing, even though there was nothing whatever remarkable about him. Except that he had blue eyes, of course.

The big man was upset; in fact, they all were. They were evidently talking about someone who was dead; it seemed like it anyhow. Now and then they would all sigh heavily, men though they were. If that was really the case, if they were mourning someone, why didn't they leave the lamenting to women, to professional mourners?

Suddenly Barabbas heard that the dead man had been crucified, and that it had happened yesterday. Yesterday . . . ?

He strained his ears to hear more, but they lowered their voices again and he could catch nothing.

Who was it they were talking about?

People were walking past out in the street and it was quite impossible to hear a word. When it was more or less quiet again, he made out enough to know it was as he thought — it was *him* they were talking about. He who . . .

How strange . . . He had been thinking about him a while ago himself. He had happened to pass the archway leading into the courtyard, and this had brought him to mind. And when passing the spot where the cross had been too much for the man, he had also thought of him. And here they were sitting talking about that very man. . . . Strange. What had they to do with him? And why did they whisper the whole time? The big red-haired man was the only one who was audible occasionally; his body didn't seem suited to whispering.

Were they saying anything about — about the darkness? About its having grown dark when he died . . .

He listened tensely, so eagerly that they must have noticed it. They suddenly fell completely silent, not uttering a word for a long time, merely sitting and looking at him out of the corners of their eyes. Then they whispered something amongst themselves which he couldn't catch. And after a while they took leave of the big man and went away. There were four of them; there was not one he liked the look of.

Barabbas was left sitting alone with the big man. He had half a mind to speak to him, but could not think how to begin. The man sat there pursing his lips, and now and then shaking his big head. As is the way with simple folk, he gave bodily expression to his troubles. At last Barabbas asked him outright what was worrying him. He looked up in perplexity with his round blue eyes without answering. But after gazing frankly at the stranger for a moment he asked if Barabbas was from Jerusalem. No, he wasn't. — But you seem to be, from your speech? Barabbas replied that his home was not so far from here, away in the mountains to the east. The man evidently found this more reassuring. He didn't trust these people here in Jerusalem, not an inch, he made no bones about it; he was sure most of them were downright robbers and scoundrels. Barabbas gave a smile and quite agreed with him. And what about himself? Himself? Oh, his home was a long, long way from here. His childlike eyes tried to express just how far away it was. And he wanted very much to be where he belonged, he confided ingenuously to Barabbas, not in Jerusalem or anywhere else in the world. But he didn't suppose he would ever get back to his native soil and live and die there as he had meant to do, as he had once imagined. Barabbas thought it sounded queer. — Why not? he asked. Who was to stop him? Isn't every man his own master?

— Oh no, the big man replied musingly. That is not so.

What was he doing here then, Barabbas could not help asking. The big man did not answer at once, but then said uncertainly that it was because of his Master.

— Master?

— Yes. Had he not heard about the Master?

— No.

— Oh. About the one who was crucified yesterday on the hill of Golgotha?

— Crucified? No, he had not heard about it. Why?

— Because it was ordained that such a thing must come to pass.

— Ordained? Was it *ordained* that he was to be crucified?

— Yes, indeed. It said so in the scriptures and, besides, the Master himself had foretold it.

— Had he? And it said so in the scriptures? Well, personally, he was not so familiar with them that he knew of it.

— No, nor am I. But that's how it is.

Barabbas did not doubt it. But how was it that his Master had to be crucified and what was the point of it anyway? It was all very strange.

— Yes, that's what I think. I can't see why he had to die. And in such a horrible way. But it had to be as he had prophesied. It must all come to pass as it was ordained. And he used to say so many times, he added, bowing his great head, that he must suffer and die for us.

Barabbas glanced up at him.

— Die for us!

— Yes, in our stead. Suffer and die, innocent, in our stead. For you have to admit that we are the guilty ones, not he.

Barabbas sat gazing out into the street and asked no more for a time.

— It is easier now to understand what he meant, the other man said to himself.

— Did you know him well? Barabbas enquired.

— Yes, indeed. Indeed, I did. I was with him from the very first moment he began up there amongst us.

— Oh, did he come from the same part as you?

— And since then I've been with him the whole time, wherever he went.

— Why?

— Why? What a question! It's easy to see you don't know him.

— What do you mean?

— Well, you see, he had power over one. A remarkable power. He would merely say to one: follow me, and one had to follow. There was nothing else to be done. Such was his power. If you had known him you would have experienced it. You too would simply have followed him.

Barabbas sat for a moment in silence. Then he said:

— Yes, he must have been an extraordinary man, if all you say is true. But surely the fact that he was crucified proved that he had no special power?

— Oh no, you're wrong there. I thought so too at first — and that's what is so terrible. That I could believe such a thing for one moment! But now I think I understand the meaning of his shameful death, now that I've thought things over a bit and talked to the others, who are more at home with the scriptures. You see, it's like this, he had to suffer all this, although he was innocent, he even had to descend into hell for our sakes. But he shall return and manifest all his glory. He is to rise again from the dead! We are quite sure of it.

— Rise from the dead? What nonsense!

— It's not nonsense. Indeed he will. Many even think it will be tomorrow morning, for that is the third day. He is supposed to have said that he would remain in hell for three days, though *I* never heard him say so. But that's what he is supposed to have said. And at sunrise tomorrow . . .

Barabbas gave a shrug.

— Don't you believe it?

— No.

— No, no . . . How can you . . . ? You who have never known him. But many of us believe. And why shouldn't he rise again himself when he has raised so many from the dead?

— Raised from the dead? That he never did!

— Yes, indeed. I've seen it with my own eyes.

— Is it really true?

— Of course it's true. Indeed it is. So he has power, all right. He has power to do anything, provided he wants to. If only he had used it for his own sake, but that he has never done. And why did he let himself be crucified if he had so much power . . . ? Yes, yes,

I know. . . . But it's not easy to grasp, I grant you.
I am a simple man, you see, it's not easy to understand all this, you may be sure.

— Are you not sure that he will rise again?

— Yes, yes, of course I am. I am quite sure it's true
what they say. That the Master is to return and reveal
himself to us in all his power and glory. I am quite
certain of that, and they know the scriptures much
better than I do. It will be a great moment. They even
say that then the new age will begin, the happy age
when the Son of Man will reign in his kingdom.

— The Son of Man?

— Yes. That's what he called himself.

— The Son of Man . . . ?

— Yes. So he said. But some believe . . . No, I
can't say it.

Barabbas moved closer to him.

— What do they believe?

— They believe . . . that he is God's own son.

— God's son!

— Yes. . . . But surely that can't be true, it's almost
enough to make one afraid. I would really much
rather he came back as he was.

Barabbas was quite worked up.

— How can they talk like that! he burst out. The

son of God! The son of God crucified! Don't you see that's impossible!

— I said that it can't be true. And I'll gladly say it again if you like.

— What sort of lunatics are they who believe that? Barabbas went on, and the scar under his eye turned dark red, as it always did when there was anything the matter. The son of God! Of course he wasn't! Do you imagine the son of God comes down onto the earth? And starts going around preaching in your native countryside!

— Oh . . . why not? It's possible. As likely there as anywhere else. It's a humble part of the world, to be sure, but he had to begin somewhere.

The big fellow looked so ingenuous that Barabbas was inclined to smile, but he was far too worked up. He twisted and turned and twitched at his goat-hair mantle the whole time as though it had slipped off one shoulder, which it hadn't.

— And the wonders that occurred at his death, the other man said, have you thought of them?

— What wonders?

— Don't you know that it grew dark when he died? Barabbas glanced away and rubbed his eyes for a moment.

— And that the earth quaked and the hill of Golgotha was rent asunder where the cross stood?

— It certainly was not! You've just made all that up! How do you know it was rent asunder? Were you there?

A sudden change came over the big man. He looked uncertainly at Barabbas and then down on the ground.

— No, no, I know nothing about it. I cannot testify to it, he stammered. And for a long time he sat silent, sighing deeply.

At last, laying his hand on Barabbas's arm, he said:

— You see . . . I was not with my Master when he suffered and died. By then I had taken to my heels. Forsaken him and fled. And before that I had even denied him. That is the very worst of all — that I *denied* him. How can he forgive me, if he returns? What shall I say, what shall I answer when he asks me about it?

And hiding his great bearded face in his hands, he rocked to and fro.

— How could I do such a thing, how is it possible for one to do such a thing . . . ?

The bright-blue eyes were full of tears when at last he raised his head again and looked at the other man.

— You asked what was troubling me. Now you know. Now you know the kind of man I am. And my Lord and Master knows even better. I am a poor miserable wretch. Do you think he can forgive me?

Barabbas answered that he thought so. He was not particularly interested in what the other man told him, but he said it all the same, partly by way of assent and partly because he could not help liking this man who sat there accusing himself like any criminal, though he had done nothing. Who hasn't let somebody else down in one way or another?

The man gripped his hand and held it tightly in his.

— Do you think so? Do you think so? he repeated in a thick voice.

At that moment a group of men walked past outside in the street. When they caught sight of the big red-haired man and saw who it was he sat talking to and holding by the hand, they started as though unable to believe their eyes. They hurried forward, and although approaching the shabbily dressed man in a curiously respectful way they burst out:

— Don't you know who that man is?

— No, he answered truthfully, I don't know. But he is a kind-hearted man and we have had a good talk together.

— Don't you know that it was in place of him that the Master was crucified?

The big man released Barabbas's hand and looked from one to the other, unable to conceal his dismay. The newcomers showed their feelings even more plainly, breathing violently in agitation.

Barabbas had got to his feet and was standing with his back turned so that his face was no longer visible.

— Get thee hence, thou reprobate! they said to him fiercely.

And pulling his mantle about him, Barabbas walked off down the street alone without looking back.

THE GIRL with the hare-lip was unable to sleep. She lay looking up at the stars and thought of what was soon to come to pass. No, she did not want to fall asleep, she wanted to keep watch this night.

She was lying on some twigs and straw she had gathered in a hollow outside the Dung Gate, and around her she could hear the sick groaning and moving restlessly in their sleep and the tinkle of the leper's bells, the one who sometimes got up and walked about because of the pain. The stench of the large refuse-heaps filled the whole valley and made it difficult to breathe, but she was so used to it that she no longer noticed it. No one here noticed it any longer.

Tomorrow at sunrise . . . Tomorrow at sunrise . . .

What a strange thought! Soon all the sick would be well and all the starving be fed. It was almost beyond belief. How would it all come about? But soon the heavens would open and the angels descend and feed them all — at least all the poor. The rich would no doubt continue to eat in their own houses, but the poor, all those who were really hungry, would be given food by angels, and here by the Dung Gate cloths would be spread out over the ground, white linen cloths, and food of all kinds would be laid out on them and everyone would lie down and eat. It wasn't really so very hard to imagine if one just thought that everything would be completely different from what it was now. Nothing would be like anything one had seen or experienced before.

Perhaps she too would be in other clothes, one never knew. White, possibly. Or perhaps in a blue skirt? Everything would be so different because the son of God was risen from the dead and the new age had dawned.

She lay thinking of it all, of how it would be.

Tomorrow . . . Tomorrow at sunrise . . . She was glad she had been told about it.

The leper's bells sounded closer at hand. She recognized them; he usually made his way up here of a night, though it was not allowed; they had to keep inside their enclosure at the very bottom of the valley, but now in the night-time he took the risk. It was as

if he sought human companionship and, for that matter, he had once said that was the reason. She saw him
picking his way between the sleepers in the starlight.

The realm of the dead . . . What was it like there
really? They said that he was now wandering about
in the realm of the dead. . . . What did it look like?
No, she had no idea . . .

The old blind man moaned in his sleep. And a little
further away the emaciated young man lay panting,
the one who could always be heard. Quite near her
lay the Galilean woman, whose arm twitched because
she had someone else's spirit in her. There were many
around her who thought they would be made whole
by the mud in the spring, and there were poor
wretches who lived on refuse from the garbage heaps.
But tomorrow no one would go rooting about there
any more. They lay twisting in their sleep, but she was
not sorry for them any more.

Perhaps the water would be purified by an angel
breathing on it? And they would really be healed
when they stepped down into it? Perhaps even the
lepers would be healed? But would they be allowed
to step down into the spring? Would they really? One
didn't know for sure how it would be. . . . No, one
knew very little really . . .

Perhaps nothing would happen to the spring and no one even bother about it. Perhaps the angelic hosts would float along through the whole Ge-Hinnom valley and over all the earth, sweeping away disease and sorrow and misfortune with their wings!

She lay thinking that perhaps that was how it would be.

Then she thought of that time when she met the son of God. Of how kind he had been to her. Never had anyone been so kind to her. She might well have asked him to cure her of her deformity, but she didn't want to. It would have been easy for him to do so, but she didn't want to ask him. He helped those who really needed help; his were the very great deeds. She would not trouble him with so little.

But it was odd, very odd, what he had said to her as she knelt there in the dust by the wayside, when he had turned and walked back to her.

— Do you too expect miracles of me? he asked.

— No, Lord, I don't. I only watched you as you passed.

Then he had given her such a tender yet sorrowful look, and he had stroked her cheek and touched her mouth without anything at all happening to it. And then he had said: — You shall bear witness for me.

How strange! What did he mean? Bear witness for me? She? It was incredible. How could she?

He had had no difficulty at all in understanding what she said, as everyone else did; he had understood at once. But it was not surprising, seeing that he was the son of God.

All kinds of thoughts came to her as she lay there. The expression of his eyes as he spoke to her and the smell of his hand as he touched her mouth . . . The stars were reflected in her wide-open eyes, and she thought how strange it was that there were more and more the longer she gazed up into the sky. Since she had stopped living in a house she had seen so many stars . . . Just what were stars anyway? She didn't know. They were created by God, of course, but what they were she didn't know. . . . Out in the desert there had been a lot of stars. . . . And up in the mountains, in the mountains at Gilgal . . . But not *that* night, no, not *that* night . . .

Then she thought of the house between the two cedar trees. . . . Her mother standing in the doorway looking after her as she walked down the hill with the curse over her. . . . Oh yes, naturally they had to turn her out and she had to live like the animals in their lairs. . . . She remembered how green the fields were that spring, and her mother standing looking after her just inside the darkened doorway to avoid being seen by the man who had uttered the curse. . . .

But it didn't matter now. Nothing mattered now.

The blind man sat up and listened; he had awakened and heard the tinkling of the leper's bells.

— Be off with you! he shouted, shaking his fist at him in the darkness. Go away! What are you doing here!

The sound of the bells died away in the night and the old man lay down again, mumbling, with his hand over his vacant eyes.

Are children who are dead also in the realm of the dead? Yes, but surely not those who die before they leave the womb? It was not possible, surely? They couldn't suffer there in torment. It couldn't be like that, surely? Though she didn't know for certain . . . Didn't know for certain about anything . . . — Cursed be the fruit of thy loins . . .

But now with the dawning of the new age perhaps all curses were lifted of themselves? It may well be. . . . Though one couldn't be sure . . .

Cursed . . . be . . . the fruit of thy loins . . .

She shivered, as though with the cold. How she longed for the morning! Wouldn't it be soon now?

She had been lying here for so long; was not the night nearly over? Yes, the stars above her were no longer the same, and the crescent moon had long since gone down behind the hills. The guard had been changed for the last time; three times now she had seen the torches up on the city walls. Yes, the night must be over. The last night . . .

Now the morning star was rising over the Mount of Olives. She recognized it at once, it was so big and clear, much bigger than all the others. Never before had she seen it shine like this. Folding her hands across her sunken breast, she lay looking up at it for a while with her burning eyes.

Then she got up swiftly and hurried away into the darkness.


He was lying crouched behind a tamarisk bush on the other side of the road, opposite the sepulchre. When it grew light he would be able to see across to it. He would have a good view of it from here. If only the sun would rise!

True, he knew that the dead man would not rise from the dead, but he wanted to see it with his own eyes to make quite sure. That was why he had got up very early, long before sunrise, and lain in wait here behind the bush. Though up to a point he was rather surprised at himself for having done so, for being here. Why was he bothering his head so much about it anyway? What had it really got to do with him?

He had expected several to be here to witness the great miracle. That was why he had hidden himself, to avoid being seen by them. But there was obviously no one else here. It was odd.

Yes, now he could make out someone kneeling a little in front of him, in the very road it seemed. Who could it be, and how had it happened? He had not heard anyone come. It looked like a woman. The grey figure was hardly discernible as it knelt there in the dust it resembled.

Now it was getting light, and soon the first rays of the sun were thrown on to the rock out of which the sepulchre was carved. It all happened so quickly that he couldn't quite follow it — now of all times when he really should have had his wits about him! The sepulchre was empty! The stone was rolled away on the ground below and the carved-out space in the rock empty!

At first he was so amazed that he merely lay staring at the opening into which he had himself seen them put the crucified man, and at the great stone which he had seen them roll in front of it. But then he realized what it was all about. Nothing had happened in actual fact. The stone had been rolled away the whole time, before ever he came. And the sepulchre had been empty even then. Who had rolled it aside and who had made off with the dead man was not hard to guess. The disciples had of course done it some time during the night. Under cover of darkness they had carried off their adored and beloved Master so as to be able to say later that he had risen from the dead just as he had predicted. It wasn't hard to work that out.

That was why there was no sign of them here this morning, at sunrise, when the miracle should really have happened. Now they were keeping out of the way!

Barabbas crept out of his hiding-place and went to inspect the sepulchre properly. As he passed the grey kneeling figure in the road he glanced down and saw to his amazement that it was the girl with the hare-lip. He stopped short, remained standing, looking down at her. Her starved ashen face was turned towards the empty sepulchre and her ecstatic eyes saw nothing else. Her lips were parted but she scarcely breathed;

the disfiguring scar in her upper lip was quite white. She did not see him.

It gave him a peculiar feeling, almost of shame, to see her like this. And he recalled something, something he didn't want to recall — that was how her face had looked then. Just as he had also had a feeling of shame then . . . He shook himself free of it.

At last she noticed him. She too seemed surprised at the meeting, that he should be here. It wasn't to be wondered at; he was surprised himself at his being here. What business was it of his?

Barabbas would have liked to pretend that he had simply been walking along the road, that he had been passing by pure chance and had no idea what place this was and that there was a sepulchre here. Could he pretend? It would seem rather far-fetched perhaps; she might not believe him, but he said all the same:

— Why are you kneeling there like that?

The girl with the hare-lip neither looked up nor moved, just went on kneeling as before, with her eyes turned towards the opening in the rock. He barely heard her whisper to herself:

— The son of God is risen . . .

It gave him a queer feeling to hear her say it. Against his will he felt something — he couldn't make out what. He stood there for a moment not knowing what to say or do. Then he went up to the sepulchre, as he had thought of doing, and made sure it was empty; but he knew that already and it meant nothing one way or the other. Then he went back to where she was kneeling. Her face was so reverent and full of rapture that he really felt sorry for her. There was no truth at all in this thing that made her happy. He could have told her all about this resurrection; but hadn't he done her enough harm already? He could not bring himself to tell her the truth. He asked her cautiously how she thought it had come to pass, how the crucified man had risen from the grave?

She looked up at him for a moment in surprise. Didn't he know? But then in her snuffling voice she described rapturously and in detail how an angel in a mantle of fire had come rushing down from heaven with arm outstretched like the point of a spear. And the spear had been thrust in between the stone and the rock and parted them. It sounded as simple as could be and it was too, although it was a miracle. That's how it had happened. Had he not seen it?

Barabbas looked down and said that he had not, and deep down inside he thought how very pleased he was not to have seen it. It showed that his eyes were all right now, like everybody else's eyes, that he no longer saw any visions but only reality itself. That man had no power over him any more; he had not witnessed any resurrection or anything. But the girl with the hare-lip still knelt there, her eyes radiant with the memory of what she had seen.

When at last she got to her feet to move away, they walked together some of the way in towards the city. They said little, but he did find out that after they had left each other that time, she had come to believe in this man she called the son of God and whom he just called the dead man. But when he asked what it was this man really taught, she was reluctant to answer. She looked away and avoided his glance. When they reached the parting of the ways — she was evidently going to take the road leading down to the valley of Ge-Hinnom while he thought of going on to the Gate of David — he asked her again what the doctrine was that he preached and which she believed in, though actually it was no concern of his. She stood for a moment looking down on the ground; then, giving him a shy look, she said in her slurring voice:

— Love one another.

And so they parted.

Barabbas stood for a long time gazing after her.

BARABBAS kept asking himself why he stayed on in Jerusalem when he had nothing to do there. He merely drifted about the city to no purpose, without turning his hands to anything. And he supposed that up in the mountains they were wondering why he was so long. Why did he stay? He didn't know himself.

The fat woman thought at first that it was because of her, but she soon realized it wasn't. She felt rather piqued, but heavens above, men are always ungrateful when they get what they want all the time, and she did have him sleeping with her and she liked that. It was lovely to have a real man for a while and one it was nice to fondle. And there was one thing about Barabbas, even if he didn't care for you, he didn't care for anyone else either; you could always be sure of that. He didn't care for anybody. He never had. And, besides, up to a point she was rather glad he didn't care for her. At any rate, while he was making love to her. Afterwards she sometimes felt a bit miserable and had a little cry all to herself. But actually she didn't mind that either. Even that could feel nice. She had great experience of love and did not disdain it in any form.

But why he mooned about here in Jerusalem was more than she could imagine. Or what he found to do all day long. It wasn't as if he were one of those good for-nothings who stood loafing about the streets; he was a man who had always been used to an active, dangerous life. It wasn't like him to dawdle around doing nothing in this way.

No, he wasn't really himself since that happened — since he was nearly crucified. He seemed to find it hard somehow to get used to the fact that he hadn't been, she told herself with a loud laugh as she lay during the worst of the midday heat with her hands across her big belly.

Barabbas could not avoid sometimes running into the followers of the crucified rabbi. No one could say that he did so deliberately; but there were a number of them here and there in the streets and marketplaces, and if he encountered them he liked to stop and talk for a while and ask them about him and that queer doctrine which he couldn't make head or tail of. Love one another? . . . He steered clear of the temple square and the fashionable streets around it and kept to the alley-ways of the lower city, where the craftsmen sat working in their shops and the hawkers cried their wares. There were many believers among these simple folk and Barabbas liked them better than those he had met up in the colonnade. He got to know something of their peculiar ideas, but he never seemed to get anywhere with them personally or understand them properly. It may have been because they expressed themselves so foolishly. They were firmly convinced that their Master had risen from the dead and that he would soon come at the head of the heavenly hosts and establish his kingdom. They all said the same; it was evidently what they had been taught. But they were not all equally sure that he was the son of God. Some thought it strange if he really were, because they themselves had both seen and heard him, even spoken to him for that matter. And one of them had made a pair of sandals for him and taken his measurements and everything. No, they found that hard to imagine. But there were many who declared that he was, and that he would sit on the heavenly throne beside the Father. But first this sinful and imperfect world would be destroyed.

What kind of queer people were they?

They noticed that he didn't for a moment believe as they did, and were on their guard against him. Some were downright suspicious and they nearly all showed that they didn't particularly like him. Barabbas was used to that, but oddly enough this time he took it to heart — which he had never done before. People had always kept out of his way and shown that they would rather not have anything to do with him. Perhaps it was because of his appearance, perhaps the knife-wound deep down into his beard which no one knew the cause of, perhaps the eyes that were so deep-set that no one could see them properly. Barabbas was quite well aware of all that, but it didn't matter to him what people thought! He had never bothered about it.

He had not known until now that it rankled.

They for their part kept together in every way through their common faith, and were very careful not to let anyone in who did not belong. They had their brotherhood and their love feasts, when they broke bread together as if they were one big family. It was probably all part and parcel of their doctrine, with their "love one another." But whether they loved anyone who was not one of themselves was hard to say

Barabbas had no wish to take part in such a love feast, not the slightest; he was put off by the very thought of such a thing, of being tied to others in that way. He wanted always to be himself and nothing else.

But he sought them out all the same.

He even pretended that he wanted to become one of them, if only he could understand their faith properly. They answered that it would make them happy and that they would gladly try and explain their Master's doctrine to him as well as they could, but in point of fact they did not appear glad. It was most odd. They reproached themselves for not being able to feel any real joy at his advances, at perhaps gaining a new fellow-believer — a thing which normally made them so happy. What could be the reason for it? But Barabbas knew why. Getting up suddenly, he strode away, the scar under his eye crimson.

Believe! How could he believe in that man he had seen hanging on a cross! That body which was long ago quite dead and which he had proved with his own eyes had not been resurrected! It was only their imagination. The whole thing was only their imagination. There wasn't anyone who rose from the dead, either their adored "Master" or anyone else! And besides, he, Barabbas, could hardly be blamed for their choice. That was their business. They could have chosen anyone at all, but it just turned out that way. The son of God! As if he could be the son of God! But supposing he were, there was surely no need for him to have been crucified if he had not wanted to be. He must have wanted it himself! There was something weird and horrid about it — he must have *wanted* to suffer. For if he really was the son of God, it would have been the easiest thing in the world to get out of it. But he didn't *want* to get out of it. He wanted to suffer and die in that dreadful way and not be spared; and so it had been; he had got his own way about not being let off. He had let him, Barabbas, go free instead. He had commanded: — Release Barabbas and crucify me.

Though of course he was not the son of God, that was obvious . . .

He had used his power in the most extraordinary way. Used it by not using it, as it were; allowed others to decide exactly as they liked; refrained from interfering and yet had got his own way all the same: to be crucified instead of Barabbas.

They spoke of his having died for them. That might be. But he really had died for Barabbas, no one could deny it! In actual fact, he was closer to him than they were, closer than anyone else, was bound up with him in quite another way. Although they didn't want to have anything to do with him. He was chosen, one might say, chosen to escape suffering, to be let off. He was the real chosen one, acquitted instead of the son of God himself — at his command, because he wished it. Though they suspected nothing!

But he didn't care for their "brotherhood" and their "love feasts" and their "love one another." He was himself. In his relationship to that crucified man they called the son of God he was also himself, as always. He was no serf under him as they were. Not one of those who went around sighing and praying to him.

How can one *want* to suffer, when there's no need, when one's not forced to? That sort of thing is beyond belief and the mere thought of it almost enough to turn the stomach. When he thought of it, he could see before him the lean, miserable body with arms hardly strong enough to hang by and the mouth that was so parched that it was all it could do to ask for a little water. No, he didn't like anyone who sought out suffering in that way, one who hung himself up on a cross. He didn't like him at all! But they adored their crucified one and his suffering, his pitiable death, which could probably never be pitiable enough for them. They adored death itself. It was horrid, it filled him with disgust. It put him right off both them and their doctrine and the one they said they believed in.

No, he didn't like death, not one bit. He loathed it and would much rather never die. Perhaps that was why he didn't have to? Why he had been chosen to be let off it? Supposing the crucified man really was the son of God, why, then he knew everything and was quite well aware that he, Barabbas, did not want to die, either suffer or die. And so he had done so in his stead! And all Barabbas had had to do was to go with him up to Golgotha and see him crucified. That was all that was asked of him and even that he had thought difficult, disliking death as he did and everything connected with it.

Yes, he was indeed the one the son of God had died for! It was to him and no other that it had been said: — Release this man and crucify me!

Such were Barabbas's thoughts as he walked away

after trying to be one of them, as he strode away from the potter's workshop in Potters' Lane, where they had so plainly shown that they did not want him among them.

And he decided to go and see them no more.

But next day, when he turned up again notwithstanding, they asked what it was in their faith that he didn't understand; showing clearly that they felt sorry and reproached themselves for not having welcomed him properly and been glad to give him the knowledge for which he was thirsting. What was it he wanted to ask them about? That he didn't understand?

Barabbas was on the point of shrugging his shoulders and replying that the whole thing was a mystery to him and, in fact, he couldn't be bothered with it. But then he mentioned that a thing like the resurrection, for instance, he found hard to grasp. He didn't believe that there was anyone who had risen from the dead.

Glancing up from their potter's wheels, they looked first at him and then at each other. And, after whispering amongst themselves, the eldest among them asked if he would like to meet a man whom their Master had raised from the dead? If so, they could arrange it, but not before the evening after work, as he lived some little way outside Jerusalem.

Barabbas was afraid. This was not what he had expected. He had imagined they would argue about it and put forward their point of view, not try and prove it in such a pushing way. True, he was convinced that the whole thing was some queer fancy, a pious swindle, and that actually the man had not been dead. He was afraid all the same. He was not a bit keen on meeting the man. But he couldn't very well say so. He must pretend he was grateful for the chance of convincing himself of their Lord and Master's power.

He put in time by walking about the streets in a state of mounting agitation. When he returned to the workshop at closing-time, a young man accompanied him out through the city gates and up towards the Mount of Olives.

The man they sought lived on the outskirts of a little village on the slopes of the mountain. When the young potter drew aside the straw mat over the doorway they saw him sitting inside with his arms in front of him on the table and gazing straight out into the room. He seemed not to notice them until the young man greeted him in his clear voice. Then he slowly turned his head towards the door and returned their

greeting in a curiously flat tone. The young man having given him a message from the brethren in Potters'
Lane and stated their errand, they were invited with
a movement of the hand to sit down at the table.

Barabbas sat opposite to him and was drawn to ex-
amine his face. It was sallow and seemed as hard as
bone. The skin was completely parched. Barabbas had
never thought a face could look like that and he had
never seen anything so desolate. It was like a desert.

To the young man's question the man replied that
it was quite true that he had been dead and brought
back to life by the rabbi from Galilee, their Master.
He had lain in the grave for four days and nights, but
his physical and mental powers were the same as before, nothing had altered as far as they were concerned. And because of this the Master had proved his
power and glory and that he was the son of God. He
spoke slowly in a monotone, looking at Barabbas the
whole time with his pale, lack-lustre eyes.

When he had finished, they continued talking for a
while about the Master and his great deeds. Barabbas
took no part in the conversation. Then the young man
got up and left them to go and see his parents, who
lived in the same village.

Barabbas had no wish to be left alone with the man,

but he could think of no pretext for abruptly taking his leave. The man looked steadily at him with the queer opaque eyes that expressed nothing at all, least of all any interest in him, but which nevertheless pulled Barabbas towards him in some inexplicable way. He would have liked to make his escape, tear himself away and escape, but he could not.

The man sat for some time without speaking. Then he asked Barabbas if he believed in their rabbi, that he was the son of God. Barabbas hesitated, then answered no, for it felt so odd to lie to those vacant eyes which didn't seem to mind in the least whether one lied or not. The man took no offence, merely said with a nod:

— No, there are many who don't. His mother, who was here yesterday, doesn't believe either. But he raised me from the dead because I am to witness for him.

Barabbas said that in that case it was only natural he should believe in him, and that he must be eternally grateful to him for the great miracle he had wrought. The man said, yes, he was, he thanked him every day for having brought him back to life, for the fact that he belonged to the realm of the dead no longer.

— The realm of the dead? Barabbas exclaimed, noticing that his voice trembled slightly. The realm of the dead? . . . What is it like there? You who have been there! Tell me what it's like!

— What it's like? the man said, looking at him questioningly. He clearly didn't quite understand what the other meant.

— Yes! What *is* it? This thing you have experienced?

— I have experienced nothing, the man answered, as though disapproving of the other's violence. I have merely been dead. And death is nothing.

— Nothing?

— No. What should it be?

Barabbas stared at him.

— Do you mean you want me to tell you something about the realm of the dead? I cannot. The realm of the dead isn't anything. It exists, but it isn't anything.

Barabbas could only stare at him. The desolate face frightened him, but he could not tear his eyes away from it.

— No, the man said, looking past him with his empty gaze, the realm of the dead isn't anything. But to those who have been there, nothing else is anything either.

— It is strange your asking such a thing, he went on. Why did you? They don't usually.

And he told him that the brethren in Jerusalem often sent people there to be converted, and indeed many had been. In that way he served the Master and repaid something of his great debt for having been restored to life. Almost every day someone was brought by this young man or one of the others and he testified to his resurrection. But of the realm of the dead he never spoke. It was the first time anyone had wanted to hear about it.

It was growing dark in the room, and, getting up, he lighted an oil lamp that hung from the low ceiling. Then he got out bread and salt, which he placed on the table between them. He broke the bread and passed some to Barabbas, dipping his own piece in the salt and inviting Barabbas to do the same. Barabbas had to do likewise, though he felt his hand shaking. They sat there in silence in the feeble light from the oil lamp, eating together.

This man had nothing against eating a love feast with him! He was not so particular as the brethren in Potters' Lane, and made but little distinction between one man and another. But when the dry, yellow fingers passed him the broken bread and he had to eat it, he imagined his mouth was filled with the taste of corpse.

Anyway, what did it mean, his eating with him like this? What was the hidden significance of this strange meal?

When they had finished, the man went with him to the door and bade him go in peace. Barabbas mumbled something and hastily took his leave. He strode rapidly out into the darkness and down the mountainside, thoughts pounding in his head.

The fat woman was joyously surprised at his violence as he took her; it was with no little zest he did it this evening. What caused it, she didn't know, but tonight it seemed as if he really needed something to hold onto. And if anyone could give that to him, she could. She lay dreaming she was young again, and that someone loved her . . .

Next day he kept clear of the lower part of the city and Potters' Lane, but one of them from the workshop there ran into him up in Solomon's colonnade and immediately asked how it was yesterday, whether it was not true what they had said? He answered that he did not doubt that the man he had visited had been dead and then resurrected, but that to his way of thinking their Master had had no right to raise him from the dead. The potter was dumbfounded, his face turning almost ashen at this insult to their Lord, but Barabbas merely turned his back and let him go.

It must have become known not only in Potters' Lane, but in the oil-pressers', the tanners', the weavers' lanes, and all the others; for when Barabbas, as time went on, went there again as usual, he noticed that the believers he usually talked to were not at all as before. They were taciturn, and looked at him suspiciously the whole time out of the corners of their eyes. There had never been any intimacy between them, but now they openly showed their mistrust. In fact a wizened little man whom he didn't even know tugged at him and asked why he was forever mixing with them, what he wanted of them, whether he was sent by the temple guard or the high priest's guard or perhaps by the Sadducees? Barabbas stood there speechless, looking at the little old man, whose bald head was quite red with rage. He had never seen him before and had no idea who he was, except that he was obviously a dyer, judging from the red and blue strands of wool stuck through holes in his ears.

Barabbas realized that he had offended them and

that their feelings towards him were quite changed. He was met with snubs and stony faces wherever he went, and some stared hard at him as if to make clear to him that they intended finding out who he was. But he pretended to take no notice.

Then one day it happened. It ran like wildfire through all the lanes where the faithful lived, suddenly there was not one who didn't know it. It is he! It is he! He who was released in the Master's stead! In the Saviour's, in God's son's stead! It is Barabbas! It's Barabbas the acquitted!

Hostile glances pursued him, hate gleamed from smouldering eyes. It was a frenzy which did not even abate after he had vanished from their sight, never to show himself there again.

— Barabbas the acquitted! Barabbas the acquitted!

H E CREPT into his shell now and didn't speak to a soul. For that matter, he hardly ever went out; just lay inside the curtain at the fat woman's or in the arbour up on the roof when there was too much of a hubbub in the house. Day after day he would spend in this manner, without occupying himself in any way whatsoever. He scarcely bothered about eating, at least he wouldn't have done if food had not been put before him and his attention drawn to it. He seemed utterly indifferent to everything.

The fat woman could not make out what was wrong with him; it was beyond her. Nor did she dare ask, either. It was best to leave him in peace, which was what he seemed to want. He barely answered when spoken to, and if one peeped cautiously inside the curtain now and again, he merely lay there staring up at the ceiling. No, it was quite beyond her. Was he going off his head? Losing his reason? It was more than she could say.

Then she hit on it. It was when she overheard that he had been mixing with those lunatics who believed in the fellow who had been crucified when Barabbas himself should have been! Then it dawned on her! No wonder he had grown a bit queer. They were the cause of it. They, of course, had been filling his head with their crazy notions. It was enough to make anyone touched, going about with half-wits like them. They thought that that crucified man was some sort of saviour or whatever it was, who was to help them in some way and give them everything they asked for, and wasn't he to be king in Jerusalem too and send the beardless devils packing? Oh, she didn't really know what it was they taught and she didn't care either, but they were soft in the head, everyone knew that. How, in heaven's name, could he go and get tied up with them? What had he to do with them? Yes! Now she had it! He himself was to have been crucified, but then he hadn't been, their saviour had been instead, and that was terrible, of course; he had to try and explain it, and so on, that it wasn't his fault, and so on. and then they had kept on talking of how remarkable that fellow was that they believed in, how pure and innocent and what an important person, if you please, and how awful it was to treat such a great king and lord in that way, had in fact filled his head with all sorts of stuff and nonsense, until he had gone quite daft because he wasn't dead, because it wasn't he who was dead. That was it, of course, that's what had happened, of course!

She might have known it was because he had not been crucified! The simpleton! She really had to laugh, laugh outright at her silly old Barabbas. He was too funny for words. Yes, that's what it was all about, of course.

But even so it was about time he pulled himself together and listened to reason. She'd have a talk with him, that she would. What was all this nonsense?

But she didn't have a talk with him. She meant to, but nothing ever came of it. For some reason one didn't start talking to Barabbas about himself. One meant to, perhaps, but could never bring oneself to do it.

So things went on as before, with her going around wondering what on earth was the matter with him. Was he ill? Perhaps he was ill? He had got thin, and the scar from the knife-wound that that Eliahu had given him was the only spot of colour in the wan, hollow face. He was a sorry sight, not at all his usual self. Not at all his usual self in any way. It wasn't like him to go mooning about like this, to lie staring up at the ceiling. Barabbas! A man like Barabbas!

Supposing it was not he? Supposing he'd become someone else, was possessed by someone else, by someone else's spirit! Just think if he were no longer himself! It certainly seemed like it! By that other man's spirit! He who really had been crucified! And who certainly wished him no good. Fancy if that "saviour" when he gave up the ghost breathed it into Barabbas instead, so as not to have to die and so as to be avenged for the wrong that had been done him, be avenged on the one who was acquitted! It was quite possible! And when one came to think of it, Barabbas had been queer like this ever since then. Yes, she remembered his strange behaviour when he had come in here just after his release. Yes, that's what it was, all right, and that explained everything. The only thing that wasn't quite clear was how the rabbi had managed to breathe his spirit into Barabbas, for he had given up the ghost at Golgotha and Barabbas had not been there. But then if he was as powerful as they made out, he could probably do even that, could make himself invisible and go wherever he wanted. He no doubt had the power to get exactly what he wanted.

Did Barabbas himself know what had happened to him, that he had someone else's spirit in him? That he himself was dead but that the crucified man was alive in him? Did he?

Perhaps he suspected nothing; but it was easy to see he was the worse for it. And no wonder, either; it was someone else's spirit and it wished him no good.

She felt sorry for him, she could hardly bear to look at him, she felt so sorry for him. He, for his part, never looked at her at all, but that was because he couldn't be bothered. He took no notice of her at all, not the slightest, so it was no wonder he didn't look at her. And he never wanted her any more at nights; that was the worst of all. It showed more than anything else that he couldn't be bothered with her. It was only she who was stupid enough to cling to this poor wretch. She would lie crying to herself of a night, but now it didn't feel a bit nice. Strange . . . She never thought to experience anything like that again.

How was she to get him back? How was she to cast out the crucified man and get Barabbas to be Barabbas again? She had no idea how you cast out spirits. She knew nothing at all about it, and this was a powerful and dangerous spirit, she could see that; she was almost afraid of it, though normally she was not of a timid nature. You only had to look at Barabbas to see how powerful it was, how it just took complete control of a big strong man who was alive himself until a short time ago. It was beyond her. No wonder she felt a bit scared. It was sure to be specially powerful having belonged to a crucified man.

No, she wasn't afraid exactly. But she didn't like crucified people. It was not in her line. She had a large, generously proportioned body, and the one that suited her was Barabbas. Barabbas as he was *himself*. Such as he was before he had got it into his head that it was he who should have been crucified. What she relished was the very fact that he had *not* been crucified, that he had got off!

Such were the fat woman's thoughts in her great loneliness. But at last it came to her that in actual fact she knew nothing at all about Barabbas. Neither what was wrong with him nor whether he was possessed by that crucified man's spirit or not. Nothing at all. All she knew was that he took no notice of her and that she was foolish enough to love him. The thought of this made her cry, and she lay there feeling dreadfully unhappy.

Barabbas was about in the city once or twice during the time he lived with her, and on one occasion it happened that he found himself in a house that was merely a low vault with vent-holes here and there to let in the light, and with a pungent smell of hides and acids. It was evidently a tannery, though it was not in Tanners' Lane but down below the temple hill towards the Vale of Kedron. Presumably it was one of those that tanned the hides of the sacrificial animals from the temple; but it was no longer in use. The vats and tubs along the walls were empty, though they still retained all their fumes and smells. The floor was littered with oak-bark, refuse and filth of all kinds that one trod in.

Barabbas had slunk in unobserved and was huddled in a corner near the entrance. There he squatted, looking out over the room full of praying people. Some he couldn't see; in fact the only ones discernible were those who happened to be lying where the light filtered through the vent-holes in the arched roof; but there must have been people lying everywhere praying, even in the semi-darkness, for the same mumbling could be heard from there too. Now and then the murmur would rise and grow stronger in one part, only to subside again and mingle with the rest. Sometimes everyone would begin praying much more loudly than before, with more and more burning zeal, and someone would get up and begin witnessing in ecstasy for the resurrected Saviour. The others would then stop speaking instantly and all turn in that direction, as though to draw strength from him. When he had finished they would all start praying together again, even more fervently than before. In most cases Barabbas could not see the witness's face, but once, when it was someone quite close to him, he saw that it was dripping with sweat. He sat watching the man in his transports, and saw how the sweat ran down the hollow cheeks. He was a middle-aged man. When he had finished he threw himself down on the earthen floor and touched it with his forehead, as everyone does in prayer; it was as though he had suddenly remembered there was also a God, not only that crucified man he had been talking about the whole time.

After him a voice could be heard a long way off which Barabbas seemed to recognize. And when he peered in that direction he found it was the big red-bearded man from Galilee standing there in a ray of light. He spoke more calmly than the others and in his native dialect, which everyone in Jerusalem thought sounded so silly. But all the same they listened more tensely to him than to anyone else. They hung on his words, though, as a matter of fact, there was nothing in the least remarkable about what he said. First he spoke for a while about his dear Master, never referring to him as anything else. Then he mentioned that the Master had said that those who believed in him would suffer persecution for his sake. And if this did happen, they would endure it as well as they could and think of what their Master himself had suffered. They were only weak, miserable human beings, not like him, but even so they would try and bear these ordeals without breaking faith and without denying him. That was all. And he seemed to say it as much to himself as to the others. When he had finished it was almost as if those present were rather disappointed in him. He noticed it, evidently, and said that he would say a prayer which the Master had once taught him. This he did, and they appeared more satisfied; some, in fact, were really moved. The whole room was filled with a kind of mutual ecstasy. When he came to the end of the prayer, and those nearest him turned as if to "congratulate" him, Barabbas saw that he was surrounded by the men who had said: "Get thee hence, thou reprobate!"

Once or two others then witnessed and were so filled

with the spirit that the congregation continued in its exaltation and many rocked their bodies to and fro as though in a trance. Barabbas watched them from his corner, sitting and taking note of everything with his wary eyes.

All at once he gave a start. In one of the beams of light he saw the girl with the hare-lip standing with her hands pressed against her flat chest and her pallid face turned up to the light that was streaming down on it. He had not seen her since that time at the sepulchre and she had become even more emaciated and wretched, clad only in rags and her cheeks sunken in from starvation. Everyone present was looking at her and wondering who she was, no one knew her apparently. He could see that they thought there was something odd about her, though they couldn't say what; except that she had nothing on but rags, of course. They were evidently wondering what her evidence would be.

What did she want to witness for? What was the point! exclaimed Barabbas within himself. Surely she realized she wasn't fitted for it. He was quite worked up, though it was nothing whatever to do with him. What did she want to witness for?

It didn't seem as though she herself were so very

happy about it, either. She stood with her eyes closed, as if unwilling to look at anyone around her and anxious to get it over. What did she want to do it for then? When there was no need . . .

Then she began to witness. She snuffled out her faith in her Lord and Saviour, and no one could possibly think there was anything moving about it, as there was presumably meant to be. On the contrary, she spoke even more absurdly and thickly than usual, because of standing in front of so many people and being nervous. And they showed clearly that they were ill at ease, that they thought it was embarrassing; some turned away in shame. She finished by snivelling something about "Lord, now I have witnessed for thee, as thou didst say I should do," and then sank down again on the earthen floor and did her best to make herself inconspicuous.

They all looked self-consciously at each other; it was as if she had ridiculed what they were about. And perhaps she had. Perhaps they were quite right. Their only thought after this seemed to be to put an end to their meeting as soon as possible. One of the leaders, one of those who had said, "Get thee hence, thou reprobate!", got up and announced that they would disperse now. And he added that everyone knew why they had met here this time and not right in the city, and that next time they would meet somewhere else, none as yet knew where. But the Lord would be sure to find a refuge for them where they could be safe from the world's evil; he would not desert his flock, he was their shepherd and . . .

Barabbas heard no more. He had crept out before the others and was glad to be well away from it all.

The mere thought of it made him feel sick.

WHEN the persecutions began, the old blind man, led by the youth who was always panting, went to one of the prosecutors in the sanhedrin and said:

— Among us out at the Dung Gate there is a woman who is spreading heresies about a Saviour who is to come and change the whole world. All that exists shall be destroyed and another and better world arise, where only his will shall be done. Should she not be stoned?

The prosecutor, who was a conscientious man, told the blind man to give more detailed reasons for his accusation. First and foremost, what kind of Saviour was he? The old man said that it was the same one that those others had been stoned for believing in, and if there was any justice then she ought to be stoned too. He himself had heard her say that her Lord would save all people, even the lepers. He would heal them and make them just as clean as the rest of us. But what would happen if the lepers became like other people? If they went about all over the place — perhaps even without having to carry bells any longer — so that no one would know where they were, at least no one who was blind. Was it lawful to spread such heresies?

Some little way from him in the darkness he could hear the councillor stroking his beard. He was then asked if there were any who believed in what she proclaimed?

— Indeed there are, he answered. Among that scum out there by the Dung Gate there are always those who are ready to listen to such things. And the lepers down in the valley like it best of all, of course. She hob-nobs with them, what is more; several times she has been inside the enclosure and taken the most shameful interest in them, it is said. She may even have had intercourse with them, for all I know. I wouldn't know anything about that. But she's no virgin anyway, from what I hear. And she is supposed to have had a child which she killed. But I don't know. I just hear what's said. There's nothing wrong with my hearing; it's only my eyes that are missing, so I am blind. And that is a great misfortune, noble Lord. A great misfortune to be blind like this.

The councillor asked if that "Saviour" as she called him — who should really be called the crucified man — had gained many adherents out there amongst them through her?

— Yes, he had. They all want to be healed, you see, and he heals them all, she says — lame, moonstruck and blind — so that there will be no more misery left in the world, either at the Dung Gate or anywhere else. But latterly they have started getting angry out there because he never comes. She's been saying for so long now that he will come, but when he never does they get annoyed of course and mock her and abuse her, and it's not to be wondered at either and nothing to lie and snivel about at night so that a body can't sleep. But the lepers still cling to it, and it's not surprising the way she has dinned it into them. She has even promised them that they shall be allowed into the temple square and go up into the Lord's house.

— The lepers!

— Yes.

— How can she promise anything so absurd?

— Well, she's not the one who does the promising,

but her Lord, and he is so powerful that he can promise anything at all and change anything at all. He sees
to everything, for he is the son of God.

— The son of God!

— Yes.

— Does she say that he is the son of God?

— Yes. And that's sheer blasphemy, because everyone knows he was crucified, and I shouldn't think
there's any need to find out any more. Those who sentenced him surely knew what they were doing, didn't
they?

— I myself was one of those who sentenced him.

— Oh, well then, you know all about him!

There was silence for a while; all the old man heard
was the councillor there in the darkness stroking his
beard again. Then the voice declared that the woman
would be summoned before the council to answer for
her faith and defend it if she could. The old man expressed his thanks and withdrew, bowing meekly;
then began scrabbling on the wall to find the doorway
by which he had come in. The councillor sent for his
attendant to help him out; but, while they were waiting, he asked the blind man, for safety's sake, if he
bore a grudge against the woman in question.

— Bear her a grudge? No. How could I? I have

never borne anyone a grudge; why should I? I have never even seen them. Not a single soul have I ever seen.

The attendant helped him out. In the street outside the entrance stood the youth from the Dung Gate, panting in the darkness; the blind man groped for his hand and they went home together.

When the girl with the hare-lip had been sentenced she was led out to the stoning-pit that lay a little to the south of the city. A whole crowd of yelling people went with her and a subordinate officer of the temple guard with his men; they, with their plaited hair and beards, were stripped to the waist and had iron-studded ox-hide whips with which to maintain order. When they reached the pit the inflamed mob spread out along the edge, while one of the soldiers led her down into it. The whole pit was full of stones, which down at the bottom were dark with old blood.

The commanding officer called for silence and a deputy of the high priest pronounced sentence and the reasons for it, saying that he who had accused her was to cast the first stone. The old blind man was led forward to the edge and told what it was all about, but he would not hear of it.

— Why should I cast stones at her? What have I to do with her? I have never even seen her!

But when at last they made him understand that such was the law and that he couldn't get out of it, he muttered crossly that he supposed he'd have to. A stone was put into his hand and he threw it out into the darkness. He tried again, but there was no point in it, as he had no idea where the target was; he merely threw straight out into the darkness which was the same in all directions. Barabbas, who was standing beside him and who up till now had had eyes only for the girl down there whom the stones were going to hit, now saw a man step forward to help the blind man. The man had a stern, aged, withered face and on his forehead he wore the law's commandments enclosed in leather capsules. He was presumably a scribe. Taking the blind man's arm he tried to aim for him, so that they could get on with the stoning. But the result was the same as before. The stone went wide of the mark. The sentenced woman was still standing down there with wide, shining eyes waiting for what was to happen.

The true believer grew so impatient at last that he bent down and picked up a large sharp stone, which he hurled with all his senile might at the hare-lipped girl. It did in fact hit her, and she staggered and raised her spindly arms in a rather helpless way. The mob gave a wild shriek of approval and the true believer stood looking down at his work, clearly well pleased with it. Barabbas, stepping right up to him, lifted his mantle slightly and stuck a knife into him with a deft movement that bespoke long practice. It happened so quickly that no one noticed anything. And, besides, they were all so busy casting their stones down on to the victim.

Barabbas pushed his way through to the edge, and there, down in the pit, he saw the girl with the hare-lip stagger forward a step or two with outstretched hands, crying out:

— He has come! He has come! I see him! I see him! . . .

Then she fell to her knees, and it was as though she seized hold of the hem of someone's garment as she snuffled:

— Lord, how can I witness for thee? Forgive me, forgive . . .

Then sinking down on the blood-stained stones she gave up the ghost.

When it was all over, those immediately around discovered that a man lay dead amongst them, while another man was seen to run off between the vineyards and disappear into the olive-groves over towards the Vale of Kedron. Several of the guard gave chase, but were unable to find him. It was as if the earth had swallowed him up.

WHEN darkness fell, Barabbas crept back to the stoning-pit and climbed down into it. He could see nothing, and had to grope his way. Right at the bottom he found her lacerated body, half buried under stones that had been cast quite needlessly, long after she was dead. It was so small and light that he hardly felt it in his arms as he carried it up the steep slope and away into the darkness.

He carried it hour after hour. Now and then he would stop and rest for a while, with the dead girl lying in front of him on the ground. The clouds had blown away and the stars were shining; after a time the moon rose too, so that everything was visible. He sat looking at her face, which oddly enough was hurt very little. Nor was it much paler than when she was alive, for this was hardly possible. It was quite transparent, and the scar in the upper lip had become so small, as though it didn't in the least matter. And it didn't either, not now.

He thought of the time when he had hit on the idea of saying that he loved her. When he had taken her — no, he put that out of his mind . . . But the time when he had said that he loved her, so that she would not give him away but do just as he wanted — how her face had lighted up. She was not used to hearing that. It seemed to make her happy in some way to hear it, though she must have known it was a lie. Or hadn't she known? In any case he had got things the way he wanted them; she had come every day with what he needed to keep himself alive, and he had got her, of course — more than he wanted really. He had made do with her because there was no other woman to hand, though her snuffling voice had got on his nerves and he had told her not to talk more than she had to. And when at last his leg was healed he had gone off again, of course. What else was he to do?

He looked out across the desert opening up before him, lifeless and arid, lit by the moon's dead light. It extended like this in all directions, he knew. He was familiar with it without having to look about him.

Love one another . . .

He glanced at her face again. Then lifting her up he resumed his way over the mountains.

He was following a camel- and mule-track that led from Jerusalem across the Desert of Juda to the land of the Moabites. There was nothing to be seen of the track itself; but droppings from animals, and occasionally the skeleton of one of them picked clean by the vultures, showed where it twisted and turned. When he had been walking for more than half the night the path began to lead downwards and he knew that he had not much further to go. He made his way down through one or two narrow clefts and then out as though into another desert, but even wilder and more desolate. The track continued across it, but he sat down to rest for a while first, tired after the strenuous descent with his burden. Anyway, he was nearly there now.

He wondered whether he would be able to find it himself or whether he would have to ask the old man. He would much prefer not to look him up, would rather do all this alone. The old man might not understand why he had brought her here. Did he understand himself, for that matter? Was there any point in it? Yes, she belonged here, he thought. That is, if she belonged anywhere at all? Down in Gilgal she would never be allowed to rest, and in Jerusalem she would have been thrown to the dogs. He didn't think she ought to be. Though what did it matter really? What difference did it make to her? What good did it do her to be brought here where she had lived as an exile and where she could find rest in the same grave as the child? None at all. But he felt he wanted to do it all the same. It is not so easy to please the dead.

What was the use of her having gone off like that to Jerusalem? Of joining those crazy desert fanatics who raved about the coming of a great messiah and said they must all make their way to the Lord's city. Had she listened to the old man instead, this would never have happened to her. The old man wasn't going to unsettle himself; he said he had done it so many times for nothing, that there were so many who made out they were the Messiah but who weren't at all. Why should it be the right one this particular time? But she listened to the madmen.

Now here she lay, battered and dead for his sake. The right one?

Was he the right one? The saviour of the world? The saviour of all mankind? Then why didn't he help her down there in the stoning-pit? Why did he let her be stoned for his sake? If he was a saviour, why didn't he save!

He could have done that all right if he'd wanted to. But he liked suffering, both his own and others'. And he liked people to witness for him. "Now I have witnessed for thee, as thou didst say I should do". . . "Risen from hell in order to witness for thee". . .

No, he didn't like that crucified man. He hated him. It was he who had killed her, had demanded this sacrifice of her and seen to it that she didn't escape it. For he had been present down there, she had seen him and gone towards him with outstretched hands for help, had snatched at his mantle — but not a finger had he lifted to help her. And he was supposed to be the son of God! God's loving son! Everyone's Saviour!

He himself had knifed that man who had cast the first stone. He, Barabbas, had done that much at least. True, it meant nothing. The stone was already cast, it had already hit her. There was absolutely no point in it. But all the same . . . He had knifed him, all the same!

He wiped his hand across his wry mouth and smiled scornfully to himself. Then he shrugged and got to his feet. Lifted up his burden, impatiently, as though he had begun to tire of it, and started off again.

He passed the old man's hermit's-cave, which he easily recognized from that time when he had come here by chance. Then he tried to remember where they had gone when the old man showed him the way to the child's grave. They had had the lepers' caves on their right and the desert fanatics' straight in front, but they hadn't gone as far as that. Yes, he recognized it quite well, though it looked different now in the moonlight. They had been walking down here towards the hollow while the old man told him that the child was still-born because it had been cursed in the womb and that he had buried it at once as everything still-born is unclean. Cursed be the fruit of thy loins . . . The mother had not been able to be present, but later on she had often sat there by the grave. . . . The old man had talked the whole time. . . .

It should be somewhere here, surely? Shouldn't it? Yes, here was the stone slab. . . .

Lifting it up, he laid her down beside the child, who was already completely withered. Arranged her torn body, as though to make sure she would be comfortable, and finally threw a glance at the face and the scar in the upper lip which didn't matter any more. Then he replaced the slab and sat down and looked out over the desert. He sat thinking that it resembled the realm of death, to which she now belonged; he had carried her into it. Once there, it made no difference really where one rested, but now she lay beside her withered child and nowhere else. He had done what he could for her, he thought, stroking his red beard and smiling scornfully.

Love one another . . .

WHEN Barabbas came back to his own people he was so changed that they scarcely recognized him. Their companions who had been down in Jerusalem had said that he seemed a bit queer; and no wonder either, being in prison for so long and then so nearly crucified. It would soon wear off, they thought. But it had not done so, not even now, so long afterwards. What lay at the back of it all was more than they could say, but he was no longer himself.

He had always been queer, of course. They had never really understood him or known just where they were with him, but this was something else. He was just like a stranger to them and he too must have thought they were strangers he had never seen before. When they explained their plans he paid hardly any attention, and he never offered any opinion himself. He seemed completely indifferent to it all. He took part, of course, in their beats along the caravan routes and the raids down the Jordan Valley now and then, but rather half-heartedly and without being of much use. If there was any danger he didn't exactly keep out of the way, but very nearly. Perhaps even this was due to sheer apathy; there was no telling. He didn't seem in the mood for anything. Only once, when they plundered a wagon with tithes from the Jericho region for the high priest, did he run completely amuck and cut down the two men from the temple guard who were escorting it. It was quite unnecessary, as they made no resistance and gave in the minute they saw they were outnumbered. Afterwards he even outraged their bodies, behaving so incredibly that the others thought it was going too far and turned away. Even if they did hate all those guards and the whole of the high priest's pack, the dead belonged to the temple and the temple belonged to the Lord. It almost frightened them, his violating them like that.

But otherwise he never showed any desire to join in and do his bit, as they all had to do; what they were up to was somehow no concern of his. Not even when they attacked a Roman picket at one of the ferry-stations by the Jordan did he show any particular enthusiasm; though it was the Romans who had wanted to crucify him and all the rest of them had been in a state of savage excitement, cutting the throats of every single soldier and flinging the bodies into the river. Not that they doubted that his hatred of the oppressors of the Lord's people was as great as theirs, but had they all been as half-hearted as he, things would have gone very badly for them that night.

The change that had come over him was quite unaccountable, for if any of them had been daring, it was Barabbas. He it was who used to plan most of their ventures and be the first to carry them out. Nothing seemed impossible for him, and he used to pull it off too. Because of his boldness and cunning they were quite willing to let him have his way and devise plans for them, and they had grown used to relying on everything turning out well. He became a kind of leader, though they didn't recognize leaders among them and no one really liked him. Perhaps it was for that very reason; because he was queer and moody and different from themselves, so that they never quite made him out and he remained a kind of stranger. They knew what they were like themselves, but where he was concerned they knew hardly anything; and oddly enough it gave them confidence. Even the fact that they were actually a little afraid of him secretly gave them confidence. Though of course it was chiefly because of his mettle and craftiness and success in what he undertook.

But now, what did they want with a leader who showed not the slightest wish to lead, who didn't even seem to want to do his share, as they all must? Who preferred to sit by the mouth of the cave staring down over the Jordan Valley and away across the sea that was called the Dead. Who looked at them with his curious eyes and in whose company they always felt ill at ease. He never really spoke to them, or if he did they only felt more than ever that there was something odd about him. He seemed to be somewhere else entirely. It was almost unpleasant. Perhaps it was part and parcel of what he had been through down in Jerusalem, of being so nearly crucified. In fact it was almost as if he really had been crucified and had then come back here again just the same.

He spread unease around him. They weren't at all pleased at having him there, at his return. He didn't belong here any longer. As leader he was impossible, and he was hardly fitted for anything else. In that case, he wasn't anything at all then? No, it was curious — he wasn't anything at all.

Now that they came to think of it, he had not always been the one who led and made decisions, not always the bold, reckless Barabbas who snapped his fingers at danger and death and everything. He had not been like that until Eliahu had given him that cut under the eye. Before then he had been anything but a dare-devil — the reverse, in fact. They remembered that very well, as a matter of fact. But after this he had suddenly become a man. After that treacherous thrust, which had really been aimed to kill, and after the savage death-struggle that followed, which had ended by Barabbas hurling the terrible but already senile and clumsy Eliahu down the precipice below the mouth of the cave. The younger man was so much more lithe and agile; despite all his strength the old warrior could not hold his own against him, and that fight was his doom. Why did he provoke it? Why did he always hate Barabbas? They had never been able to find out. But they had all noticed that he had done so from the first moment.

It was after this that Barabbas had become their leader. Up till then there had been nothing special about him. He had not become a real man until he had got that knife-wound.

So they sat talking, whispering amongst themselves. But what they did not know, what nobody at all knew, was that this Eliahu, who now stood out so clearly and vividly in their minds, was Barabbas's father. No one knew that, no one could know. His mother was a Moabite woman whom the band had taken prisoner many years before when they plundered a caravan on the Jericho highway and with whom they had all amused themselves before selling her to a brothel in Jerusalem. When it became obvious that she was pregnant, the proprietress wouldn't keep her there any longer and sent her packing, and she gave birth in the street and was found dead afterwards. Nobody knew whom the child belonged to, and she couldn't have said herself; only that she had cursed it in her womb and borne it in hatred of heaven and earth and the Creator of heaven and earth.

No, nobody knew the ins and outs of it. Neither the whispering men right at the back of the cave, nor Barabbas as he sat at the opening, gazing out into the void across to the burnt-up mountains of Moab and the endless sea that was called the Dead.

Barabbas was not even thinking of Eliahu, although he was sitting just where he had flung him down the rock-face. He was thinking instead, for some reason — or rather, for no reason at all — of the crucified Saviour's mother, of how she had stood looking at her nailed-up son, at him she had once borne. He remembered her dry eyes and her rough peasant's face which couldn't express the grief she felt, and perhaps didn't want to, either, amongst strangers. And he remembered her reproachful look at him as she passed. Why just at him? There were surely plenty of others to reproach!

He often thought of Golgotha and what had happened there. And often of her, that other man's mother . . .

He looked away again over the mountains on the other side of the Dead Sea, and saw how the darkness came down over them, over the land of the Moabites.

THEY wondered greatly how they could get rid of him. They longed to be free of this useless and irksome encumbrance and to be spared the sight of his gloomy face, which depressed them and made everything so joyless. But how were they to go about it? How could it be done, how could they say to his face that he didn't fit in here any longer and that they would be glad if he took himself off? Who was going to tell him? None of them was particularly keen; to be quite honest, none of them dared. For no reason, they were still possessed by a kind of absurd fear.

So they continued with their whispering; saying how fed up with him they were and how they disliked him, and always had; and that it was perhaps his fault that they were starting to be dogged by such bad luck and had recently lost two men. They could hardly expect much luck with a Jonah like that amongst them. A sultry and menacing feeling of tension filled the cave, and eyes that were almost malevolent glittered in the semi-darkness at the man who sat brooding alone out by the precipice, as though bound to an evil destiny. How were they to get rid of him!

And then one morning he had simply disappeared. He just wasn't there. They thought at first that he had lost his reason and thrown himself over the cliff, or that an evil spirit had entered into him and flung him into space. Perhaps Eliahu's spirit, to be avenged on him? But when they searched down below in the same spot where they had once found Eliahu's battered body, he was not there, nor could they find the slightest trace of him anywhere. He had simply disappeared.

Feeling greatly relieved, they returned to their eyrie up on the steep mountain-side, which was already burning-hot from the sun.

OF BARABBAS's fate, where his haunts were and what he did with himself after these events and during the rest of his manhood, no one knows anything for certain. Some think that after his disappearance he retired into complete solitude somewhere in the desert, in the desert of Judah or the desert of Sinai, and devoted himself to the contemplation of the world of God and mankind; while others think that he joined the Samaritans, who hated the temple in Jerusalem and the priesthood and the scribes there, that he is supposed to have been seen during the Passover on their holy mountain at the sacrificing of the lamb, kneeling, waiting for the sunrise at Gerizim. But some regard it as proven that for the greater part of the time he was simply the leader of a robber band on the slopes of Lebanon, towards Syria, and as such showed cruelty to both Jews and Christians who fell into his hands.

As has been said, no one can know which of these is true. But what is definitely known is that when well into his fifties he came as a slave to the Roman governor's house in Paphos after having spent several years in the Cyprian copper mines which were subject to the latter's administration. Why he had been seized and condemned to the mines, to the most ghastly punishment imaginable, is not known. But more remarkable than the fact that such a thing could happen to him is that once having descended to this hell he was ever able to return to life again, though still a slave. There were, however, special circumstances connected with this.

He was now a grey-haired man with a furrowed face but otherwise remarkably well preserved, in view of all he had gone through. He had recovered amazingly soon and regained much of his strength. When he left the mines he resembled a dead man rather than a living one; his body was quite emaciated and his eye-sockets expressionless, like wells that have been drained dry. When the expression in his eyes returned, it became even more restless than before, and uneasy, dog-like, as though cowed; but it also glittered occasionally with the hatred his mother felt for all creation when she gave birth to him. The scar under his eye, which had faded right away, once more dug down into the grey beard.

Had he not been of such tough material he would never have survived. He had Eliahu and the Moabite woman to thank for this; they had once again given him life. And this despite their both having hated, not loved, him. Nor had they loved each other. That is how much love means. But he knew nothing of what he owed them and their malevolent embrace.

The house to which he came was large, with many slaves. Among them was a tall, lanky, very lean man, an Armenian called Sahak. He was so tall that he always walked with a slight stoop. His eyes were large, a trifle protuberant, and his dark, wide-eyed gaze made him glow in some way. The short white hair and the burnt-up face made one think he was an old man, but actually he was only in his forties. He too had been in the mines. Barabbas and he had spent their years there together, and together had succeeded in getting away. But he had not recovered like the other one; he was still just as incredibly emaciated, and the snow-white hair and seemingly fire-ravaged face gave him a branded and scorched appearance that made him look quite different. He seemed to have under-gone something which Barabbas, in spite of every-thing, had not endured. And this was indeed so.

The other slaves were very curious about these two who had managed to escape from something which normally no one got out of alive, and they would have liked very much to hear all about it. But they did not get much out of them regarding their past. The two kept to themselves, though they did not speak much to each other either, nor did they seem to have very much in common. Yet even so they appeared inseparable in some way. It was strange. But if they always sat next to each other during meals and their time off, and always lay beside each other in the straw at night, it was only because they had been chained together in the mines.

This had been done the moment they arrived in the same transport from the mainland. The slaves were shackled together in twos and then the same pair always worked together side by side in the depths of the mine. Neither was ever separated from his fellow-prisoner, and these twin slaves did everything in common and grew to know one another inside out, sometimes to the point of frenzied hatred. They had been known to hurl themselves at each other in savage fury for no reason other than that they were welded together like this in hell.

But these two seemed to suit each other and even to help each other endure their servitude. They got on well together and were able to talk, in this way diverting themselves during the heavy work. Barabbas was not very communicative, of course, so the other did most of the talking, but he liked to listen. They did not speak of themselves to begin with, neither of them seemed to want to; they both evidently had their secrets which they were unwilling to reveal, so it was some time before they really knew anything about each other. It was more by chance one day that Barabbas happened to mention he was a Hebrew and born in a city called Jerusalem. Sahak was extraordinarily interested when he heard this, and began asking about one thing and another. He seemed to be quite familiar with this city, although he had never been there. At last he asked if Barabbas knew of a rabbi who had lived and worked there, a great prophet in whom many believed. Barabbas knew who was meant and answered that he had heard about him. Sahak was eager to know something about him, but Barabbas replied evasively that he did not know so very much. Had he himself ever seen him? Yes, he had, as a matter of fact. Sahak attached great importance to the fact that Barabbas had seen him, for after a while he asked once more if it were really true that he had done so. And Barabbas again replied, though rather half-heartedly, that he had.

Sahak lowered his pick and stood deep in thought, stood there completely absorbed by what had happened to him. Everything had become so different for him; he could scarcely realize it. The whole mine-shaft was transfigured and nothing was the same as before. He was chained together with one who had seen God.

As he stood there he felt the lash of the slave-driver's whip whine across his back. The overseer had just happened to pass by. He crouched down under the blows, as if thereby to avoid them, and began zealously swinging the pointed pick. When his tormentor finally passed on he was covered in blood and the whole of his long body was still quivering from the lashes. Some time elapsed before he could speak again, but when he did he asked Barabbas to tell him how it was he had seen the rabbi. Was it in the temple, in the sanctuary? Was it one of the times when he spoke of his future kingdom? Or when was it? At first Barabbas would not say, but at last he answered reluctantly that it was at Golgotha.

— Golgotha? What is that?

Barabbas said that it was a place where they crucified criminals.

Sahak was silent. He lowered his eyes. Then he said quietly:

— Oh, it was *then* . . .

This is what happened the first time they talked about the crucified rabbi, which they were often to do later on.

Sahak wanted very much to hear about him, but especially about the holy words he had uttered and about the great miracles he had performed. He knew, of course, that he had been crucified, but he would rather Barabbas told him about something else.

Golgotha . . . Golgotha . . . Such a strange, unfamiliar name for something that was nevertheless so well-known to him. How many times had he not heard of how the Saviour had died on the cross and of the wondrous things that had happened then. He asked Barabbas if he had seen the veil of the temple after it had been rent? And the rock too had been cleft asunder — he must have seen that since he was standing there at that very moment?

Barabbas replied that it might well have happened, though he had not seen it.

— Yes, and the dead who had got up out of their graves! Who had risen from the realm of death in order to witness for him, for his power and glory!

— Yes . . . Barabbas said.

— And the darkness that descended over all the earth when he gave up the ghost?

Yes, Barabbas had seen *that*. He had seen the darkness.

It seemed to make Sahak very happy to hear this, though at the same time he did appear to be worried by the thought of that place of execution; he could almost see in front of him the cleft rock and the cross standing upon it, with the son of God hung up to be sacrificed. Yes, of course, the Saviour had to suffer and die, he had to do that in order to save us. That's how it was, though it was hard to understand. He preferred to think of him in his glory, in his own kingdom, where everything was so different from here. And he wished that Barabbas, to whom he was fettered, had seen him another time and not at Golgotha. How was it he saw him there of all places?

— That you should see him just then, he said to Barabbas, wasn't that rather strange? Why were you there?

But to this Barabbas made no reply.

Once Sahak asked if he really had not seen him at some other time as well. Barabbas did not answer at once. Then he said that he had also been present in the courtyard of the palace when the rabbi was condemned, and described all that had happened. He also mentioned the extraordinary light that he had seen surrounding him on that occasion. And when he

111

noticed how happy it made Sahak to hear about this light, he did not bother to mention that it was only because he had been dazzled by the sun, coming straight out into it from the dungeon. Why should he mention it? It was of no interest to the other — it was of no interest to anyone. By not bothering to give an explanation of the miracle, he made Sahak so happy that he wanted to hear all about it over and over again. His face shone and even Barabbas felt something of his happiness; it was as though they shared it. Whenever Sahak asked him, he would tell him about his wonderful vision, now so long ago, imagining he saw it clearly in front of him.

Some time later he confided to Sahak that he had also witnessed the Master's resurrection. No, not so that he had seen him rise from the dead, no one had done that. But he had seen an angel shoot down from the sky with his arm outstretched like the point of a spear and his mantle blazing behind him like a flame of fire. And the point of the spear had rolled away the stone from the tomb, pushing in between the stone and the rock and parting them. And then he had seen that the tomb was empty. . . .

Sahak listened in amazement, his large ingenuous eyes fastened on the other. Was it possible? Was it really possible that this wretched, filthy slave had seen this happen? That he had been present when the greatest of all miracles occurred? Who was he? And how was it he himself was so favoured as to be shackled to one who had experienced this and been so close to the Lord?

He was beside himself with joy at what he had heard, and felt that now he must confide his secret to the other, he could no longer contain it. Glancing around cautiously to make sure that no one was coming, he whispered to Barabbas that he had something to show him. He led him over to the oil-lamp burning on a ledge in the rock-face, and by its flickering light showed him the slave's disk which he wore round his neck. All slaves wore a similar disk, on which their owner's mark was stamped. The slaves here in the mine bore the mark of the Roman State on their disks, for it was to this they belonged. But on the reverse of Sahak's disk they could together make out several strange, mysterious signs which neither of them could interpret but which Sahak explained meant the name of the crucified one, the Saviour, God's own son. Barabbas looked in wonderment at the curious notches which seemed to have a magic significance, but Sahak whispered that they meant he belonged to the son of

God, that he was his slave. And he let Barabbas himself touch it. Barabbas stood for a long time holding
it in his hand.

For a moment they thought they heard the overseer
coming, but it was not so, and they leant against each
other once more to look at the inscription. Sahak said
that it had been done by a Greek slave. He was a
Christian, and had told him about the Saviour and his
kingdom that was soon to come; he it was who had
taught him to believe. Sahak had met him at the
smelting-furnaces, where none can survive for more
than a year at the very most. The Greek had not survived so long, and as he breathed his last there in the
glowing heat Sahak had heard him whisper: — Lord,
do not forsake me. They had chopped off his foot to
remove the shackles more easily and thrown him into
the furnace, as they always did in such cases. Sahak
had expected to end his life in the same way; but not
long afterwards a number of slaves, Sahak amongst
them, had been removed here, where more were
needed.

Now Barabbas knew that he too was a Christian
and that he was God's own slave, Sahak finished, looking at the other man with his steadfast eyes.

Barabbas was very reticent and quiet for several

days after this. Then he asked Sahak in a curiously faltering voice if he would not engrave the same inscription on his disk too.

Sahak was only too pleased, providing he could. He did not know the secret signs, but he had his own disk to copy from.

They waited their chance until the overseer had just gone by, and with a sharp splinter of stone Sahak, by the light of the oil-lamp, began engraving the signs as well as he could. It was not easy for him with his unpractised hand to copy the strange outlines, but he took pains to do his very best and make it as similar as possible. Many times they had to break off because someone was coming, or because they fancied so, but at last it was finished, and they both thought it was really quite like. Each stood looking in silence at his inscription, at the mysterious signs which they understood nothing at all about, but which they knew signified the crucified man's name — that they belonged to him. And suddenly they both sank down on their knees in fervent prayer to their Lord, the Saviour and God of all oppressed.

The overseer saw them from some distance away, lying as they were right up near the lamp, but they themselves noticed nothing, so engrossed were they in their prayer. He rushed up and flayed them half to death. When at last he moved on Sahak sank to the ground, but the man then turned back and forced him up again with further lashes. Staggering against each other, they resumed their work.

This was the first time Barabbas suffered for the crucified man's sake, for that pale-skinned rabbi with no hair on his chest who had been crucified in his stead.

So the years passed. Day after day. They would not have been able to tell one day from another had they not been shoved away every evening to sleep together with hundreds of others who were equally exhausted, and from this realized that it was night. They were never allowed to leave the mine. Like shadows, blood-less, they lived perpetually, year after year, in the same semi-darkness down there in their realm of death, guided by the flickering lamps and here and there by a log-fire. Up by the mouth of the pit a little daylight forced its way down, and there they could look up towards something that might be the sky. But they could see nothing of the earth, of the world to which they had once belonged. There too, at the mouth of the mine, food was lowered to them in baskets and dirty troughs, from which they fed like animals.

Sahak had a great sorrow. Barabbas no longer prayed with him. He had done so once or twice after wanting to have the Saviour's name engraved on his slave's disk, but then never again. He had merely become more and more reserved and strange, impossible to understand. Sahak understood nothing. It was a complete mystery to him. He himself continued to pray, but Barabbas would only turn away, as though he did not even want to watch. He used to place himself so that he screened the other while he prayed, in case someone came along, so that Sahak would not be disturbed during his prayers. It was as though he wanted to help him pray. But he himself did not pray.

Why? What was the reason? Sahak had no idea. It was all a riddle, just as Barabbas himself had become a riddle to him. He had thought he knew him so well and that they had come so close to one another down here in the underworld, in their common place of punishment, especially when they lay and prayed together those few times. And all at once he found that he knew nothing about him, nothing at all really, although he was so attached to him. Sometimes he even felt that this strange man at his side was utterly foreign to him in some way.

Who was he?

They continued talking to each other, but it was

never the same as before, and Barabbas had a way of half turning his back when they spoke together. Sahak never again managed to see his eyes. But had he ever really seen them? Now that he thought of it — had he ever really done so?

Just whom was he chained to?

Barabbas never again spoke of his visions. The loss of this to Sahak, the emptiness, is not hard to understand. He tried to recall them as well as he could, tried to see them in front of him, but it was not easy. And it was not the same; how could it be? He had never stood by the side of the Loving One and been dazzled by the light around him. He had never seen God.

He had to content himself with the memory of something wonderful he had once seen with Barabbas's eyes.

He especially loved the vision of Easter morning, the burning angel flashing down to set the Lord free from hell. With that picture really clear before him, Sahak knew that his Lord was undoubtedly risen from the dead, that he was alive. And that he would soon return to establish his kingdom here on earth, as he had so often promised. Sahak never doubted it for a moment; he was quite certain that it would come to pass. And then they would be called up out of the mine, all who languished here. Yes, the Lord himself would stand at the very pit-head and receive the slaves and free them from their fetters as they came up, and then they would all enter his kingdom.

Sahak longed greatly for this. And each time they were fed he would stand and look up through the shaft to see if the miracle had occurred. But one could not see anything of the world up there, nor know what might have happened to it. So many wonderful things might have taken place about which one had not the faintest idea. Though they would surely have been brought up if something like that really had happened, if the Lord really had come. He would surely not forget them, not forget his own down here in hell.

Once when Sahak was kneeling at the rock-face saying his prayers something extraordinary happened. An overseer who was fairly new in the mine, and who had replaced their former tormentor, approached them from behind in such a way that Sahak neither saw nor heard him. But Barabbas, who was standing beside the praying man without praying himself, caught sight of him in the semi-darkness and whispered urgently to Sahak that someone was coming. Sahak immediately rose from his knees and his prayer and began working busily with his pick. He expected the worst, all the same, and cowered down in advance as though he already felt the lash across his back. To the great amazement of them both, however, nothing happened. The overseer did in fact stop, but he asked Sahak quite kindly why he had been kneeling like that, what it meant. Sahak stammered that he had been praying to his god.

— Which god? the man asked.

And when Sahak told him, he nodded silently as though to say that he had thought as much. He began questioning him about the crucified "Saviour," whom he had heard spoken of and had obviously pondered over a great deal. Was it really true that he had let himself be crucified? That he suffered a slave's base death? And that he was nevertheless able to make people worship him afterwards as a god? Extraordinary, quite extraordinary . . . And why was he called the Saviour? A curious name for a god . . . What was meant by it? . . . Was he supposed to save us? Save our souls? Strange . . . Why should he do that?

Sahak tried to explain as well as he could. And the man listened willingly, though there was but little clarity and coherence in the ignorant slave's explanation. Now and then he would shake his head, but the whole time he listened as though the simple words really concerned him. At last he said that there were so many gods, there must be. And one ought to sacrifice to them all to be on the safe side.

Sahak replied that he who had been crucified demanded no sacrifices. He demanded only that one sacrifice oneself.

— What's that you say? Sacrifice oneself? What do you mean?

— Well, that one sacrifice oneself in his great smelting-furnace, Sahak said.

— In his smelting-furnace . . . ?

The overseer shook his head.

— You are a simple slave, he said after a moment, and your words match your wits. What strange fancies! Where did you pick up such foolish words?

— From a Greek slave, Sahak answered. That is what he used to say. I don't really know what it means.

— No, I'm sure you don't. Nor does anyone else. Sacrifice oneself . . . In his smelting-furnace . . . In his smelting-furnace . . .

And continuing to mumble something which they could no longer catch, he disappeared into the darkness between the sparsely placed oil-lamps, like one losing his way in the bowels of the earth.

Sahak and Barabbas puzzled greatly over this striking event in their existence. It was so unexpected that they could scarcely grasp it. How had this man been able to come down here to them? And was he really an ordinary overseer? Behaving like that! Asking about the crucified one, about the Saviour! No, they could not see how it was possible, but of course they were glad about what had happened to them.

After this the overseer often stopped to speak to Sahak as he passed by. Barabbas he never spoke to. And he got Sahak to tell him more about his lord, about his life and his miracles, and about his strange doctrine that we should all love one another. And one day the overseer said:

— I too have long been thinking of believing in this god. But how can I? How can I believe in anything so strange? And I who am an overseer of slaves, how can I worship a crucified slave?

Sahak replied that his Lord had admittedly died a slave's death but that in actual fact he was God himself. Yes, the only God. If one believes in him one can no longer believe in any other.

— The only god! And crucified like a slave! What presumption! Do you mean that there is supposed to be only *one* god, and that people crucified him!

— Yes, Sahak said. That is how it is.

The man gazed at him, dumbfounded. And shaking

his head, as was his habit, he went on his way, vanishing into the dark passage of the mine.

They stood looking after him. Caught a glimpse of him for a second by the next oil-lamp, and then he was gone.

But the overseer was thinking of this unknown god who merely became more incomprehensible the more he heard about him. Supposing he really were the only god? That it were to him one should pray and none other? Supposing there were only one mighty god who was master of heaven and earth and who proclaimed his teaching everywhere, even down here in the underworld? A teaching so remarkable that one could not grasp it? "Love one another . . . love one another". . . No, who could understand that. . . ?

He stopped in the darkness between two lamps in order to consider it better in solitude. And all at once it came like an inspiration to him what he was to do. That he was to get the slave who believed in the unknown god away from the mine here, where all succumbed in the end, and have him put to some other work, something up in the sun. He did not understand this god, and still less his teaching; it was not possible for him to understand it, but that is what he would do. It felt just as though this were the god's will.

And when he was next above ground he sought out

the overseer in charge of the slaves who worked on the landed property belonging to the mine. When the latter, who was a man with a fresh peasant's face but a large, coarse mouth, realized what it was all about, he showed clearly that the idea did not appeal to him. He had no wish for a slave from the mines. In point of fact he needed several slaves, especially now with the spring ploughing, for as usual there were not nearly enough oxen to do the draught work. But he did not want anyone from the mines. They were quite useless, had no strength at all and, besides, the other slaves would have nothing to do with them. What did they want up here above ground? But in the end he let himself be persuaded by the older man, who had a strange capacity of getting his own way. And the latter returned to the mine.

The following day he talked to Sahak about his god for longer than he had ever done before. And then he told him what he had arranged for him. He was to present himself to the guard at the bottom of the shaft to be freed from his shackles and separated from his fellow-prisoner. And then he would be taken up out of the mine and put in charge of the man under whom he was to work from now on.

Sahak looked at him, unable to believe his ears.

Could it be true? The overseer said that it was, and that this had evidently been shown to him by Sahak's god in order that his will might be done.

Sahak pressed his hands to his breast and stood for a moment in silence. But then he said that he would not be separated from his fellow-prisoner, for they had the same god and the same faith.

The overseer looked at Barabbas in astonishment.

— The same faith? He? But he never kneels and prays as you do!

— No, Sahak replied, somewhat uncertainly, that may be. But he has been close to him in quite a different way, he has stood by his cross while he suffered and died on it. And he has seen a bright light around him once and an angel of fire who rolled away the stone from his tomb in order that he could rise from hell. He it is who has opened my eyes to his glory.

All this was beyond the overseer, who shook his head in a puzzled way and looked sideways at Barabbas, at the man with the scar under his eye who always avoided meeting one's glance and who even now was standing there with averted eyes. Did he belong to Sahak's god? It was not possible, surely? He did not like him.

Nor had he any wish to let him also out of the mine. But Sahak said again:

— I cannot be separated from him.

The overseer stood mumbling to himself and looking at Barabbas out of the corner of his eye. At length he agreed very reluctantly that it should be as Sahak wished and that they should keep each other company as before. Then he walked away from them into his solitude.

When Sahak and Barabbas presented themselves to the guard at the appointed time, they were both freed from their chains and taken up out of the mine. And when they came up into the daylight and saw the spring sun shining across the mountain-side that smelt of myrtle and lavender, and the green fields in the valley below and the sea beyond, Sahak fell down on his knees and cried out in ecstasy:

— He has come! He has come! Behold, his kingdom is here!

The slave-driver who had come to fetch them looked at him agape as he knelt there. Then he prodded him with his foot as a sign to get up.

— Come now, he said.

THEY were well suited for harnessing together to the plough, for they had already been coupled for so long that they were as used to each other as a pair of mules. They were gaunt and scraggy, of course, and with their half-shaven heads they were a laughing-stock among the other slaves; it was obvious at a glance where they came from. But one of them at any rate picked up again fairly soon; he was a robust fellow by nature, and after a while they pulled together quite well. The overseer was reasonably satisfied with them; they were not so bad, considering that they were prisoners from the mine.

They themselves were full of gratitude for what had happened to them. Even though they had to toil like oxen from morning till night, it was still so different from before. Just being out in the air, being able to breathe it, made everything so much easier. They delighted in the sun, though their lean bodies dripped with sweat and they were treated just like cattle and really no better than before. The lash whined over them as it had done in the mine, especially over Sahak, who was not as strong as Barabbas. But they had nevertheless returned to life, as it were; they lived on the earth like other beings and not down in perpetual darkness. Morning and evening came, day and night, and they were there to see it and know the joy of it. But they were well aware that God's kingdom had not yet come.

By degrees the other slaves changed their attitude towards them and ceased to regard them as some curious kind of animal. Their hair grew again and they became like all the others, and less notice was taken of them. The remarkable thing about them really was not that they had been prisoners in the mine, but that they had been able to escape from the hell to which they were condemned. In actual fact it was this that had, from the very beginning, aroused the others' curiosity and a kind of reluctant admiration, though they wouldn't own to it. They tried to get out of the other two how it had all come about, but were not very successful. The newcomers were not talkative, and regarding this miracle they didn't seem to want to talk at all. They were a bit odd and kept mostly to themselves.

They need not have done so now. They were no longer chained together. They could have made friends with some of the others if they had wanted to, and there was no further need to eat and sleep beside each other. But they still stuck together and always walked close beside each other as if inseparable. It was all the more strange as in point of fact they had grown shy of one another and found talking more difficult now. They acted as inseparable, though they had drifted apart.

While working they had to go side by side. But not at other times, when they could have mixed with the other slaves. Feeling out of it as they did, however, perhaps it was not really so odd that they held aloof. They had grown so used to keeping together, and used to the chain that was no longer there. When they woke up in the dark at night and felt that they were not shackled together they were almost frightened, until it dawned on them that at least they were lying side by side as before. The knowledge was a relief.

To think that Barabbas should live to see such a thing! That it could be like that for him! It was most extraordinary. For if anyone was ill-suited to being hobbled together with another person, it was he. Against his will, however, he had been; with an iron chain, what is more. And even though the chain no longer existed he still retained it in one way; couldn't do without it, apparently. Though of course he tugged at it in an effort to break away. . . .

But not Sahak. On the contrary, he felt very hurt that things were not as before between them. Why weren't they?

Of their miraculous rescue from the mines, from hell, they never spoke. The first day or two they had done so, but not after that. Sahak had said then that they had been rescued by the son of God, everyone's Saviour. Yes, they had . . . Of course they had . . . Though in actual fact it was Sahak who had been rescued by his Saviour, by the son of God, but Barabbas had been rescued by Sahak. Wasn't that right? Wasn't that how it was?

Hm, it was hard to say.

Barabbas had in any case thanked Sahak for saving him. But had he thanked God? Yes, surely he had? But it wasn't certain. One couldn't be sure.

It grieved Sahak that he knew so infinitely little about Barabbas, whom he was so fond of. And it hurt him so much that they were unable to pray together, as they had done down in the mine, in hell. How he would have loved to do it! But he didn't reproach him. He just didn't understand.

There was so much about Barabbas that one didn't understand. But anyway it was he who had seen the Saviour die, and rise again from the dead; and the heavenly light all around him he had seen too. Though they never talked about that any more. . . .

Sahak grieved—but not for his own sake. His gaunt, burnt-up face beneath the snow-white hair was scarred by sparks from the smelting-furnaces and the lash had wealed his emaciated body. But for his own part he did not grieve. For his own part he was, on the contrary, a happy man. Especially now, since his Lord had worked this miracle for him, brought him up here into the sun and up to the lilies of the field, which he himself had spoken of so beautifully.

He had worked the same miracle for Barabbas too. But Barabbas gazed uneasily about him in the world that lay again before his eyes, and none knew what he was thinking.

Such was their relationship during the first part of their time up there.

When the spring ploughing was finished they were put to work the water-wheels which must be set going as soon as the heat began, if everything was not to get dried up. This too was heavy work. And later, when the harvest had been got in, they were moved down to the corn-mill, one of the many buildings which surrounded the Roman governor's residence and made, together with the dirty native village, an entire little town around the shipping-port. In this way they had come right down to the sea.

It was there, inside the mill, that they met the little one-eyed man.

He was a thick-set slave with short-cropped head and a grey, wrinkled face with a shrivelled mouth. His one eye had a furtive look, the other had been gouged out because he had once stolen some bushels of flour. For this reason too he had a large wooden frame round his neck. His job was to fill the sacks with flour and carry them into the store-room, and neither this simple task nor his mouse-coloured, insignificant appearance was in the least remarkable. For some reason he was more conspicuous than most of the others all the same, perhaps because one felt so strangely insecure and ill at ease in his presence. One always knew if he was there or not, and even without turning around his one-eyed stare could be distinctly felt. It was seldom one came face to face with him.

He paid no attention whatever to the two new-comers; he didn't even appear to see them. It passed quite unnoticed that he observed with a slight sneer that they were assigned to the heaviest millstone. No one could possibly see that he smiled, that his grey, withered-up mouth meant to smile. There were four mills and each was worked by two slaves. It was customary for asses to be used, but they were less plentiful here than humans, of whom there were more than enough and who were also cheaper to keep. But Sahak and Barabbas thought that the food here was almost plentiful compared with what they had been used to, and that by and large they were better off now than before, in spite of the heavy work. The slave-driver did not treat them so badly; he was a stout, rather easy-going man who mostly went about with his whip over his back without using it. The only one to whom he used to give a taste of it was an old blind slave who was practically on his last legs.

The whole building inside was white with flour which had settled everywhere in the course of the years, on the floor and the walls and on all the cobwebs in the ceiling. The air was thick with flour-dust and filled with the hollow rumble of the millstones as they were revolved in all four mills at once. All the slaves worked naked, except the little one-eyed man, who wore a loin-cloth of sacking and sneaked about inside the flour-mill like a rat. The wooden frame around his neck gave him the appearance of having been trapped but of having broken loose in some way. It was said that he ate flour out of the sacks when he was alone in the store-room, though the wooden frame was supposed to prevent this. And that he did it not from hunger but in defiance, because he knew that if he were caught he would have the other eye put out and would be set to pull the millstone, just like the old blind man — work that he knew was more than he could manage and which filled him with almost as great a horror as the darkness which awaited him if they caught him stealing again. But how much of this was true it was hard to say.

No, he was not specially interested in the two new-comers. He watched them on the sly, as he watched all the others, and waited to see what would happen. He had nothing special against them. Nothing *special*. They were prisoners from the mine, he had heard. He had never come across any before. But he had nothing special against mine-prisoners. He had nothing special against anybody.

Seeing that they had been in the copper mines, they

must be dangerous criminals, though one of them hardly looked like it. By comparison the other did, and was evidently anxious to conceal it. He was a contemptible type and the other was a simpleton, but how had they got out of the mine? Up out of hell? Who had helped them? That was the point. But it was nothing to do with him.

If one waits long enough something always turns up. An explanation is always forthcoming in one way or another. Everything explains itself, so to speak. One has to keep an eye open, of course. And this he did.

So it was that he saw the tall lean one with the big cow-eyes kneel down at night in the darkness and pray. Why did he do that? He was praying to a god of course, but which? What sort of god did one pray to in that way?

The little one-eyed man knew of many gods, though it would never have occurred to him to pray to them. And had the idea by any chance struck him, he would naturally have done as everyone else did, prayed before their image in the temple to which they belonged. But this curious slave prayed to a god who, he obviously thought, was there in the darkness in front of him. And he spoke to him just as he would to a living being, who, he imagined, took notice of him. It was most peculiar. He could be heard whispering and praying earnestly there in the dark, but anybody could see that there was no god there. It was all imagination.

One can't very well be interested in what doesn't exist, but after making this discovery the one-eyed man began talking to Sahak now and then to find out more about this extraordinary god. And Sahak explained it all to him as well as he could. He said that his god was everywhere, even in the dark. One could call on him anywhere at all and feel his presence. Why, one could even feel him inside one's own breast, and that was the most blissful of all. The one-eyed man answered that it was really a remarkable lord he had.

— Yes, it is indeed, said Sahak.

The one-eyed man seemed to ponder a while over what he had heard, over Sahak's invisible but obviously very powerful god, and then he asked if it was he who had helped them to get out of the mine?

— Yes, Sahak said. It was.

And he added that he was the god of all the oppressed and was going to free all slaves from their chains and redeem them. For Sahak wanted to proclaim his faith and felt that the other was longing to hear this.

— Oh? said the one-eyed man.

Sahak realized more and more that the little slave, whom no one could be bothered with and whose eye had been put out, wanted to hear about his and everyone's salvation, and that it was the Lord's will that he should speak to him about it. He therefore did so as often as possible, though Barabbas looked askance at them and seemed to disapprove. And at last, one evening when they were sitting by themselves on one of the millstones after the day's work, he showed him his secret, the inscription on the back of his slave's disk. It all really came about through the one-eyed man's asking the unknown god's name — provided this might be uttered — and then Sahak had told it to him, and to prove his Lord's power and greatness had let him see the actual secret signs that stood for the holy name. The one-eyed man regarded the inscription with great interest and listened to Sahak's story of the Greek slave who had engraved it and had understood the meaning of every stroke. It was incredible how anyone in his way could know the sign of god.

Sahak looked once more at the inscription and then

turned it inwards again. And as he held it to his breast he said joyously that he was God's own slave, that he belonged to him.

— Oh, said the one-eyed man.

And after a while he asked if the other one from the mines also had this inscription on his slave's disk.

— Why, yes, said Sahak.

And the little man nodded and said yes, of course, though actually he had not been at all sure that they had quite the same faith and the same god, for this criminal with the gash under his eye never prayed. They went on talking of this strange god, and did so several more times after this conversation, which Sahak felt had brought them very close to one another. He had done right in confiding his great secret to the other and it was surely the Lord himself who had inspired him to do so.

Great was the amazement in the mill when the slave-driver one morning announced that Sahak and Barabbas were summoned to appear before the governor himself at a certain time during the day. It was the first time such a thing had happened, at any rate in this slave-driver's day, and he was just as amazed as any of the others and was quite at a loss to know what lay behind it all. Two wretched slaves in the actual presence of the Roman governor! He was to conduct them there and seemed a little anxious himself, as he had never before set foot inside the mighty one's residence. However, it was hardly likely that he could have anything to do with the matter; he was only responsible for their getting there. At the appointed time they set off, and everyone in the mill stood gazing after them, even the little slave who resembled a rat and who couldn't smile because he had a shrivelled-up mouth — he too stood gazing after them with his one eye.

Sahak and Barabbas would not have been able to find their own way through the narrow streets, which were completely strange to them. They followed immediately behind their slave-driver and kept close together, just as before. It was as if they had been chained together again.

Arrived at the great house, they were admitted through the carved cedar-wood doors by a magnificent black slave who was fettered to the door-post. He merely showed them into the vestibule and handed them over to an officer on duty, who led them across a sunny courtyard to a medium-sized room that opened on to it. There they suddenly found themselves face to face with the Roman.

All three flung themselves down on their faces and touched the floor with their foreheads, as the slave-driver had dinned into them, though both Sahak and Barabbas considered it shameless to humble oneself like that in front of one who, after all, was only a human being. Not until they were told did they dare get up. The Roman, who was leaning back in a chair on the far side of the room, beckoned them to approach, which they did hesitantly, venturing by degrees to look up at him. He was a powerfully built man of about sixty with a plump but not flabby face, broad chin and a mouth that they quickly saw was wont to command. The eyes were sharply observant but not actually unfriendly. Oddly enough, there was nothing really frightening about him.

He enquired of the slave-driver first how the two slaves had conducted themselves, if he was satisfied with them. The man stammered out that he was, adding for safety's sake that he always treated his slaves very severely. It was impossible to know whether his noble lord appreciated this; he threw a quick glance at the man's fat body and dismissed him with a light wave of the hand — he could go. The man was far from having anything against this and instantly took his leave; in fact in his hurry he was so lacking in respect that he nearly turned his back on his lord.

The latter then turned to Sahak and Barabbas and began asking them where they came from, what they had been punished for and how they had come up out of the mine, who had arranged it. The whole time he spoke quite kindly. Then getting up, he walked across the floor, and they were surprised to find that he was so tall. Going up to Sahak, he took hold of his slave's disk, looked at the stamp on it and asked if he knew what it meant. Sahak replied that it was the stamp of the Roman State. The governor said with a nod that that was quite right, and that it therefore showed that Sahak belonged to the State. Then turning the metal disk over, he looked with evident interest, but with no sign of surprise, at the secret inscription on the back. "Christos Iesus". . . he read, and both Sahak and Barabbas were filled with wonder that he could read the signs, decipher God's holy name.

— Who is that? he asked.

— It is my god, Sahak answered with a slight tremor in his voice.

— Aha. It is a name I cannot remember having heard before. But then there are so many gods, one can't keep track of them all. Is it the god of your native province?

— No, Sahak answered. It is everybody's god.

— Everybody's? You don't say so? That's not at all bad. And I have never even heard of him. He keeps his renown somewhat secret, if I may say so.

— Yes, said Sahak.

— Everybody's god. In that case he must have more than a little power. What does he base it on?

— On love.

— Love? . . . Well, why not. Anyway, it's no concern of mine, you may believe as you like about it. But tell me, why do you bear his name on your slave's disk?

— Because I belong to him, Sahak said, again with a slight tremor.

— Indeed? Belong to him? How can you do that? Do you not belong to the State, just as this stamp signifies? Are you not a state slave?

Sahak made no reply. He merely stood looking down at the floor.

At last the Roman said, but not at all unkindly:

— You must answer this. We must be quite clear on this point, don't you see? Do you belong to the State? Tell me now.

— I belong to the Lord my God, said Sahak, without looking up.

The governor stood regarding him. Then he lifted Sahak's head and looked into his burnt-up face, the face that had been at the smelting-furnaces. He said nothing, and after a time, when he had seen what he wanted, he let go the other man's chin.

Then he went and stood in front of Barabbas, and as he turned over his slave's disk in the same way he asked:

— And you? Do you also believe in this loving god?

Barabbas made no reply.

— Tell me. Do you?

Barabbas shook his head.

— You don't? Why do you bear his name on your disk then?

Barabbas was silent as before.

— Is he not your god? Isn't that what the inscription means?

— I have no god, Barabbas answered at last, so softly that it could hardly be heard. But Sahak and the Roman both heard it. And Sahak gave him a look so full of despair, pain and amazement at his incredible words that Barabbas felt it pass right through him, right into his inmost being, even though he did not meet the other's eyes.

The Roman too seemed surprised.

— But I don't understand, he said. Why then do you bear this "Christos Iesus" carved on your disk?

— Because I want to believe, Barabbas said, without looking up at either of them.

The Roman looked at him, at his ravaged face and the gash under the eye; at the hard, coarse mouth, which still retained much of its strength. There was no expression in the face and he was not sure that he would find any there even if he lifted up the head as he had done with the other. Besides, it would never have occurred to him to do so with this man. Why? He didn't know.

He turned again to Sahak.

— Do you grasp fully the implication of what you have said? That it means you are setting yourself up against Caesar? Do you not know that he too is a god and that it is to him you belong, his stamp you bear on your disk? And you say that you belong to another, unknown god, whose name you have carved on your disk to show that you are not Caesar's but his. Is that not so?

— Yes, Sahak answered in a shaking voice, but it did not tremble as much as before.

— And you stick to this?

— Yes.

— But don't you understand what you are letting yourself in for by doing so?

— Yes. I understand.

The Roman paused, thinking of this slave's god, whom as a matter of fact he had heard spoken of quite a lot recently, this madman in Jerusalem who had himself died a slave's death. "Loose all chains" . . . "God's own slave, whom he will set free". . . Anything but a harmless doctrine, in fact . . . And faces such as that slave's had no appeal for a slave-owner. . . .

— If you renounce your faith no harm shall come to you, he said. Will you do it?

— I cannot, Sahak replied.

— Why not!

— I cannot deny my God.

— Extraordinary man . . . Surely you must be aware of the punishment you force me to sentence you to. Are you really so brave that you can die for your faith?

— That is not for me to decide, said Sahak quietly.

— That doesn't sound so very brave. Is life not dear to you?

— Yes, answered Sahak. It is.

— But if you do not forswear this god of yours, nothing can save you. You will lose your life.

— I cannot lose the Lord my God.

The Roman shrugged his shoulders.

— Then there is nothing more I can do for you, he said, going over to the table at which he had been sitting when they came. He struck its marble top with a little ivory hammer.

— You are just as crazy as your god, he added, half to himself.

While they were waiting for the guard to come, the governor went up to Barabbas, turned the slave's disk over, drew out his dagger and scratched the point of it across the words "Christos Iesus."

— There's really no need, as you don't believe in him in any case, he said.

While this was happening Sahak looked at Barabbas with an expression that seared through him like fire and which he was never to forget.

And so Sahak was led away by the guard and Barabbas was left standing there. The governor commended him for his sensible behaviour and said that he wished to reward him for it. He was to report to the foreman of the slaves here in the house and have other and better work assigned to him.

Barabbas gave him a quick look and the Roman found that the man's eyes did in fact have an expression, harmless though it was. Hatred was quivering there like the point of an arrow that would never be shot.

And so Barabbas went to do as he had been commanded.

WHEN Sahak was crucified Barabbas stood concealed behind some hibiscus bushes a little distance away, so that his friend on the cross should not be able to see him. But Sahak had already been tortured so much beforehand that he was unlikely to have been aware of him. This had been done from force of habit and because they had thought that the governor had simply forgotten to give the order. Actually the governor had not meant anything like that, though he had not bothered either to give an order to the contrary. And so for safety's sake they had done as usual. What the slave was sentenced for they had no idea, nor did they care. They were doing this sort of thing continually.

Half of his head had been shaved again and the white hair was stained with blood. The face expressed nothing, really, but Barabbas who knew it so well understood what it would have expressed had it been able. He stood gazing at it the whole time with burning eyes, if it can be said that eyes such as Barabbas's are burning, and it could be said now. He also gazed at the emaciated body; he could not have torn himself away even if he had wanted to, and he didn't want to. The body was so scraggy and feeble that it was hard to imagine what crime it could have committed. But on the chest, where every rib was visible, the State's insignia were branded, to show that it was a case of high treason. The slave's disk, on the other hand, had been removed for the sake of the metal and because it was no longer needed.

The place of execution was a small rise outside the town, surrounded here and there at the foot by one or two bushes and thickets. Behind one of these stood Barabbas the acquitted. Apart from him and those who had charge of the crucifixion there was not a soul there, no one had bothered to witness Sahak's death. Otherwise people often collected, especially when the victim was guilty of a heinous crime. But Sahak had committed neither murder nor anything else, and nobody knew him or what he had done.

It was spring again now, just as it had been when they came up out of the mine and Sahak had fallen on his knees and exclaimed "He has come!" The earth was green and even the execution-hill was full of flowers. The sun was shining on the mountains and across the sea that lay not far below. But it was the middle of the day, the heat was already oppressive and big swarms of flies rose up the moment anyone moved on the befouled slope. They were all over Sahak's body, and he was past being able to move sufficiently to drive them away. No, there was nothing great or uplifting about Sahak's death.

It was all the more curious, therefore, that Barabbas could be so moved by it. But he was. He followed it with eyes that were resolved to remember every detail — the sweat that ran down the forehead and from the deep, hollow armpits; the heaving chest with its marks from the State's branding-irons; the flies that no one chased away. The head hung down and the dying man groaned heavily, Barabbas heard every breath right down where he was standing. He too breathed jerkily and heavily, and his mouth was half-open like his friend's up there. He even thought he felt thirsty, as the other undoubtedly did. It was re-markable that Barabbas could feel as he did, but he had been shackled together with him for so long. He thought he still was, for that matter, that he and the crucified man were united again with their iron chain.

Sahak was now trying to get something out, there was something he wanted to say; perhaps he wanted a drink, but no one could catch what it was. Nor could Barabbas hear what he was saying, in spite of straining his ears. Besides, he was standing much too far away. He could, of course, have rushed up the slope, up to the cross, and cried out to his friend up there, asked what he wanted, if there was something he could do for him — and he could at the same time have chased away the flies. But he didn't. He stood there hidden behind his bush. He did nothing. He merely gazed at him the whole time with burning eyes and his mouth half-open from the other's pain.

Not so very long after this it was clear that the crucified man would not have to suffer much more. His breath came faintly; it was no longer audible down where Barabbas stood, and the chest was hardly moving. After a while it stopped altogether and one could take it that Sahak was dead. Without any dark-ness descending over the earth and without any miracles at all, he quietly and unobtrusively gave up the ghost. None of those who were waiting for him to die noticed anything; they lay playing dice just as they had done that time so long ago. But this time they did not start up and were not in the least alarmed that the man on the cross had died. They didn't even notice it. The only one who did was Barabbas. And when he realized what had happened, he gave a gasp and sank down on his knees as though in prayer.

Strange . . . And to think how happy Sahak would have been if he had lived to see it. Unfortunately he was already dead.

And anyway, even though Barabbas was kneeling, he was not in fact praying. He had no one to pray to. But he knelt there for a while all the same.

Then he hid his ravaged, grey-bearded face in his hands and seemed to cry.

Suddenly one of the soldiers uttered an oath, on discovering that the crucified man was dead and that all they had to do was to take him down and go home. And so they did.


Thus it was when Sahak was crucified and Barabbas the acquitted stood looking on.

WHEN the governor retired from his governorship and returned to Rome to spend his remaining years there, he had amassed a fortune which was greater than that of any previous ruler of the island; but at the same time he had administered the mines and the whole province with a profit to the State unknown before. Innumerable overseers and slave-drivers had contributed to this success by their sense of duty, severity and perhaps even cruelty; thanks to them it had been possible to exploit fully the natural resources and squeeze both population and slaves to the utmost. But he himself was far from cruel. It was only his rule that was hard, not himself; if anyone blamed him for such a thing it was due to ignorance, to the fact that one didn't know him. And to most people he was an unknown, half-mythical person. Thousands of human wrecks down in their

153

mine-pits and at their ploughs out in the sun-baked fields gave a sigh of relief when they heard that he thought of going away; in their simplicity they hoped that a new ruler would be better. But the governor himself left the beautiful island with sadness and regret. He had been very happy there.

He was particularly aware that he would miss his work, for he was a vigorous and active man who liked to have plenty to do. But he was also a highly cultured person and therefore looked forward at the same time to the possibilities Rome offered of a refined way of living and intercourse with cultivated equals. As he reclined in his comfortable easy chair on the shady poop deck of the ship his thoughts lingered on this with pleasure.

He had taken with him the slaves he thought he would need for his own use and, among them, Barabbas. He had, however, put him down on the list more out of consideration and sentiment, for a slave of his age was not likely to be of much use to him. But he liked this sensible slave who had loyally allowed his god's name to be crossed out, and decided that he should come too. No one could believe that Barabbas's master was so considerate and unforgetful.

The voyage took longer than usual as the ship was

greatly becalmed, but after several weeks' continuous rowing it glided into the port of Ostia with the galley-slaves bleeding, and the governor arrived in Rome the very next day, followed within a day or two by his retinue and possessions.

The palace which he had arranged to buy was in the most fashionable quarter and in the very heart of the city. It was several storeys high and decorated inside with multi-coloured marble and in every way furnished with excessive luxury. Barabbas, who lived in the basement, like all the other slaves, never saw much more of it than this, but he realized that it must be a very sumptuous and magnificent house. It was quite immaterial to him. He was given light work to do, odd jobs of various kinds, and each morning he and several of the other slaves went with the superintendent of the kitchen, a haughty freedman, when the latter made his purchases in the market. In this way he got to see quite a lot of Rome.

Perhaps it cannot be said that he really saw it. It merely flitted past his eyes without seeming to affect him. When jostled by the crowd in the narrow streets or walking about the clamorous market-places, which were so full of people that one could hardly push one's way through, it all reached him as something extraneous and as though through a mist. The mighty, tumultuous capital never, in fact, became a reality to him, and he went about absently in the midst of it, engrossed in his own thoughts. Men and women from every country and of every race were mixed higgledy-piggledy, and anyone but Barabbas would probably have been fascinated by this seething mass and by all the wealth and splendour, by the stately buildings and the innumerable temples to every imaginable god, to which the nobility had themselves carried in costly, gilded litters to worship each his own — when they did not prefer the luxury shops in the Via Sacra or one of the resplendent baths. Eyes other than his would no doubt have reflected all this, enraptured. But Barabbas's eyes reflected nothing; perhaps they were too deep-set to do so, and what they saw merely glided past like something that did not concern them. No, he didn't care a straw for this world. He was indifferent to it. So he thought himself, at any rate.

But he could not have been quite so indifferent to it as he thought, all the same. For he hated it.

Among the other things that seemed unreal to him were the many processions that passed through the streets, with their priests and believers and sacred emblems. To him who had no god it must have felt strange to be meeting them continuously and to have to make way for them. Pressed against the house walls, he watched them with a stealthy, averted look. Once he even followed one of these processions into a remarkable temple which he had never seen before, and when inside he, like the others, stopped in front of a picture of a mother with her boy-child in her arms; and when he asked who it was they said that it was the most blessed Isis with the child Horus. But then they began looking at him suspiciously, at someone who did not know the Holy Mother's name, and a temple guard came and turned him out; by the copper portal the guard made a secret sign to protect himself and the temple. Perhaps he saw that Barabbas was conceived and born in hatred of all things created in heaven and earth and of the Creator of heaven and earth.

With the scar down his cheek flaming red and the pupils of his fierce, hidden-away eyes quivering like arrow-heads, Barabbas rushed away, and then through street after street and lane after lane. Get thee hence, thou reprobate! He lost his bearings and hadn't the faintest idea where he was, and when at last he found his way home he only narrowly escaped being punished; but this they dared not do as they knew that he was in favour with the master of the house. And besides, they believed his muddled explanation that he had lost his way in the city that was still so strange to him. He crouched in his corner in the slave-cellar and as he lay there in the darkness he felt the crossed-out "Christos Iesus" burn like fire against his heaving chest.

That night he dreamt that he was shackled to a slave who lay beside him praying, but whom he could not see.

— What are you praying for? he asked him. What is the use?

— I am praying for you, the slave answered out of the darkness in a well-known voice.

Then he lay quite still so as not to disturb the praying man and felt his old eyes filling with tears. But when he awoke and fumbled about on the floor for the chain, it was not there, nor the slave either. He was not bound together with anyone. Not with anyone at all in the whole world.

On one occasion when he was alone in one of the cellars underneath the palace, he found the sign of the fish carved into the wall in an out-of-the-way place. It was clumsily done but there was no doubt as to what it was intended to be and the meaning of it. He stood wondering which of the slaves could be a Christian. He wondered greatly over it during the days and weeks that followed and observed each one of them carefully to try and find out. But he asked no one. He didn't ferret it out by making enquiries as to whether there was anyone who knew. In that case it would not have been so difficult. But he did nothing like that.

He did not associate with them, with the other slaves, more than was absolutely necessary. He never spoke to any of them and therefore didn't know them. And for this reason no one knew him or bothered about him.

There were many Christians in Rome, that he knew. He knew that they assembled in their prayer-houses, in their brotherhoods in different parts of the city. But he made no effort to go along. It may have crossed his mind once or twice, but he never went. He bore the name of their God carved on his disk, but it was crossed out.

Latterly they had apparently had to meet in secret, in other places, as they were afraid of persecution. Barabbas had heard about it in the market-place from several who had spaced out their fingers after them by way of protection, just as the temple guard in the

Holy Mother's temple had done to him. They were abhorred, hated, suspected of witchcraft and goodness knows what. And their god was a notorious malefactor who had been hanged a long time ago. Nobody wanted to have anything to do with them.

One evening Barabbas overheard two of the slaves standing whispering together in the darkness of the cellar; they could not see him and believed themselves alone. Barabbas could not see them either, but he recognized them by their voices. They were two newly-bought slaves who had not been many weeks in the house.

They were speaking of a meeting of the brethren that was to be held the following evening in Marcus Lucius' vineyard on the Appian Way. After a while Barabbas realized that it was not in the vineyard they were all to meet but in the Jewish catacombs that had their beginning there.

Curious place at which to meet . . . Among the dead . . . How could they want to meet there . . . ?

On the evening of the next day, in good time before the slave-cellar was shut for the night, he slipped away from the palace at the risk of his life.

When he came out on the Via Appia it was nearly dusk and there was scarcely any longer a soul to be seen. He found the vineyard by asking a shepherd who was driving his flock home along the road.

Once down under the earth he groped his way along in the narrow, sloping passage. The daylight from the opening still guided him as he made his way down into the first burial gallery and saw how it extended into the darkness. He groped his way along in it, feeling with his hands against the cold, damp stone slabs of the walls. They were to gather in the first big burial chamber, he had understood from the two slaves. He went on.

Now he thought he could hear voices. He stopped and listened; no, there wasn't a sound. He continued. He had to go very warily the whole time as there were often steps, one or several steps, that always led still deeper down into the earth. He went on and on.

But he didn't come to any burial chamber. It was still the same narrow gallery. Now it was branching off, he could feel, and he didn't know which way to choose. He stood hesitating, utterly at a loss. Then he saw a gleam of light in the distance, quite a long way off. Yes, it was a gleam of light! He hurried towards it. That's where it must be!

But suddenly there was no longer any light to be seen. It had vanished, perhaps because without his knowing he had turned into another passage-way, a side-passage to the first. He hurried back to see the light again. But it had disappeared; it was not there any more!

He stood there completely dazed. Where were they? Where was he to find them? Were they not here then?

And where was he himself? Oh yes, he knew how he had got here; he could always find his way back to the entrance. And he decided to return as he had come.

But as he was making his way back along the gallery which he knew he had followed the whole time and where he recognized every step up, he suddenly caught sight of the gleam of light again. A strong, unmistakable glow, but in a side-passage which he had evidently not noticed previously, and not in the same direction as before. It must be the same glow, however, and he hurried towards it. That's where it must be! The glow became brighter and brighter. . . .

Until all at once it went out. Just wasn't there. . . .

He put his hand to his head. To his eyes. Whatever kind of light was it he had seen? *Wasn't* it a light?

Was it only imagination, or something funny with his eyes, like that time long, long ago . . . ? He rubbed them and looked about him. . . .

No, there was no light here at all. Not anywhere, in any direction! Only an endless, icy darkness surrounding him, in which he was quite alone — for they were not here at all; there wasn't a soul here, a single human being other than himself, only the dead!

The dead! He was surrounded by the dead. Everywhere, in every direction, in every passage and gallery, whichever way he turned. Where was he to go? He had no idea which way he was to go in order to get out again, to get away from here, out of the realm of the dead. . . .

The realm of the dead . . . He was in the realm of the dead! He was shut up inside the realm of the dead!

He was filled with terror. A suffocating terror. And suddenly he rushed away, senselessly, panic-stricken, in any direction at all, stumbling over unseen steps, into one passage after the other, trying to find the way out, the way out of the realm of the dead. . . . He strayed about down there like a man crazed, panting and gasping for breath. . . . At last he simply swayed along the passages, bumping against the walls where all the dead lay walled up, against the walls of death, outside which he could never come. . . .

At last he felt a warm current of air from up on the earth, from another world. . . . Half insensibly, he dragged himself up the slope and came out among the grape-vines.

There he lay resting on the ground and looking up at the dark void of heaven.

It was dark now everywhere. In heaven as well as on earth. Everywhere . . .


As Barabbas made his way back to the city along the nocturnal Via Appia he felt very much alone. Not because no one walked beside him on the road and no one passed him, but because he was alone in the endless night that rested over the whole earth, alone in heaven and on earth and among the living and the dead. This he had always been, but it wasn't until now that he realized it. He walked there in the darkness, as though buried in it, walked there with the scar in his lonely old face, the scar from the blow his father had dealt him. And among the grey hairs on his wrinkled chest hung his slave's disk with God's crossed-out name. Yes, he was alone in heaven and on earth.

And he was immured in himself, in his own realm of death. How could he break out of it?

Once and once only had he been united to another, but that was only with an iron chain. Never with anything else but an iron chain.

He heard his own footsteps against the stone surface of the road. Otherwise the silence was complete, as though there were not another living soul in all the world. On all sides he was surrounded by the darkness. Not a light. Not a light anywhere. There were no stars in the heavens and all was desolate and void.

He breathed heavily, for the air was sultry and hot. It felt feverish — or was it he who was feverish, who was ill, who had got death into him down there? Death! He always had that inside him, he had had that inside him as long as he had lived. It hunted him inside himself, in the dark mole's passages of his mind, and filled him with its terror. Although he was so old now, although he had no wish to live any longer, it still filled him with its terror just the same. Although he wanted so much — just wanted . . .

No, no, not to die! Not to die! . . .

But they gathered down there in the realm of the

dead to pray to their God, to be united with him and with each other. They were not afraid of death; they had vanquished it. Gathered for their fraternal meetings, their love feasts . . . Love one another . . . Love one another . . .

But when he came they were not there, not a single one of them was there. He simply wandered around alone in the dark, in the passages, in his own mole's passages. . . .

Where were they? Where were they who made out that they loved one another?

Where were they this night, this sultry night . . . ? Now that he had entered the city it felt even more oppressive — this night that was brooding over the whole world — this night of fever in which he could scarcely breathe — which was stifling him. . . .

As he turned a street-corner he felt the smell of smoke strike against him. It was coming from the cellar of a house not far away; the smoke was billowing out of the basement and from one or two vent-holes tongues of flame came licking out. . . . He hurried towards it.

As he ran he heard cries all around him from other running people:

— Fire! Fire!

At a street-crossing he found that it was also burning in a side-street, burning even more fiercely there. He grew bewildered, couldn't understand . . . Then suddenly he heard shouts some distance away:

— It's the Christians! It's the Christians!

And from one side after the other:

— It's the Christians! It's the Christians!

At first he stood there dumbfounded, as if unable to take in what they said, what they meant. The Christians . . . ? Then he understood, then he got it.

Yes! It's the Christians! It's the Christians who are setting fire to Rome! Who are setting fire to the whole world!

Now he knew why they had not been out there. They were here to set this odious Rome, to set the whole of this odious world on fire! Their hour had come! Their Saviour had come!

The crucified man had returned, he of Golgotha had returned. To save mankind, to destroy this world, as he had promised. To annihilate it, let it go up in flames, as he had promised! Now he was really showing his might. And he, Barabbas, was to help him! Barabbas the reprobate, his reprobate brother from Golgotha, would not fail. Not now. Not this time. Not now! He had already rushed up to the nearest blaze, snatched up a brand and run and flung it down into the window of a cellar in another house. He fetched one brand after the other and ran and flung them down in new places, in new cellars. He did not fail! Barabbas did not fail! He set light well and truly. No half measures! The flames leapt out of one house after the other, scorching all the walls; everything was burning. And Barabbas rushed on, to spread the fire still more, rushed around panting with God's crossed-out name on his chest. He did not fail. He did not fail his Lord when he really needed him, when the hour was come, the great hour when everything was to perish. It was spreading, spreading! Everything was one vast sea of fire. The whole world, the whole world was ablaze!

Behold, his kingdom is here! Behold, his kingdom is here!

IN THE prison underneath the Capitol all the Christians who had been accused of the fire were collected, and among them Barabbas as well. He had been caught red-handed and, after interrogation, had been taken there and thrown together with them. He was one of them.

The prison was hewn out of the actual rock and the walls dripped with moisture. In the prevailing half-light they could not see each other very distinctly and Barabbas was glad of it. He sat by himself in the rotting straw rather to one side, and the whole time with his face averted.

They had spoken a lot about the fire and the fate that awaited them. Their having been accused of starting the fire must have been merely a pretext to arrest and sentence them. Their judge knew perfectly well that they had not done it. Not a single one of them had been there; they had not gone outside their doors after they had had warning that there was to be a persecution and that their meeting-place in the catacombs had been betrayed. They were innocent. But what did that matter? Everyone wanted to believe them guilty. Everyone wanted to believe what had been shouted out in the streets by the hired mob: "It's the Christians! It's the Christians!"

— Who hired them? said a voice from out of the darkness. But the others took no notice.

How could the Master's followers be guilty of such a thing as arson, of setting Rome on fire? How could anyone believe such a thing? Their Master set human souls on fire, not their cities. He was the Lord and God of the world, not a malefactor.

And they began speaking of him who was Love and the Light and of his kingdom which they were awaiting, according to his promise. Then they sang hymns with strange and lovely words which Barabbas had never heard before. He sat with bowed head listening to them.

The iron-studded bar outside the door was drawn aside, there was a squeaking of hinges and a jailer came in. He left the door open to admit more light during the prisoners' feeding, of which he had charge.

He himself had clearly just had his dinner and regaled himself liberally with wine, for he was red-faced and talkative. Uttering coarse words of abuse, he tossed them the food they were to have; it was almost un-eatable. He didn't mean any harm with his swearing, however; he was merely speaking the language of his trade, the one that all jailers used. He sounded almost good-natured, as a matter of fact. On catching sight of Barabbas, who happened to be sitting full in the light from the doorway, he gave a bellow of laughter.

— There's that crazy loon! he shouted. The one who ran around setting fire to Rome! You half-wit! And then you all say it wasn't you who set light to every-thing! You're a pack of liars! He was caught in the act of hurling a brand down into Caius Servius' oil-store.

Barabbas kept his eyes lowered. His face was rigid and expressed nothing, but the scar under his eye was burning red.

The other prisoners turned to him, amazed. None of them knew him. They had thought he was a criminal, one who didn't belong to them; he had not even been interrogated or put into prison at the same time as they had.

— It's not possible, they whispered among themselves.

— What isn't possible? asked the jailer.

— He can't be a Christian, they said. Not if he has done what you say.

— Can't he? But he has said so himself. Those who caught him told me so, they told me everything. And he even confessed it at the interrogation.

— We do not know him, they mumbled, uneasy. And if he belonged to us, then surely we ought to know him. He's an utter stranger to us.

— You're all a nice lot of humbugs! Wait a minute, you'll soon see!

And going up to Barabbas he turned over his slave's disk.

— Take a look at this — isn't that your god's name all right? I can't make out this scrawl, but isn't it, eh? Read for yourselves!

They crowded around him and Barabbas, gaping in astonishment at the inscription on the back of the disk. The majority of them couldn't decipher it either, but one or two whispered in a subdued and anxious tone:

— Christos Iesus . . . Christos Iesus . . .

The jailer flung the disk back against Barabbas's chest and looked around triumphantly.

— Now what do you say, eh? Not a Christian, eh? He showed it to the judge himself and said that he didn't belong to the emperor but to that god you pray to, the one who was hanged. And now he'll be hanged too, that I can swear to. And all the rest of you, for that matter! Though you were all much more cunning about it than he was. It's a pity that one of you was stupid enough to go running straight into our arms saying he was a Christian!

And grinning broadly at their bewildered faces, he went out, slamming the door behind him.

They crowded again around Barabbas and began plying him furiously with questions. Who was he? Was he really a Christian? Which brotherhood did he belong to? Was it really true that he had started the fire?

Barabbas made no answer. His face was ashen grey and the old eyes had crept in as far as possible so as not to be seen.

— Christian! Didn't you see that the inscription was crossed out?

— Was it crossed out? Was the Lord's name crossed out?

— Of course it was! Didn't you see?

One or two had seen it but hadn't given it a second thought. What did it mean anyway?

One of them snatched at the slave's disk and peered at it once more; even though the light was worse now, they could still see that the inscription was scratched out with a clear, rough cross apparently made with a knife by some powerful hand.

— Why is the Lord's name crossed out? they asked, one after the other. What does it mean? Don't you hear? What does it mean!

But Barabbas didn't answer even now. He sat with his shoulders hunched and avoided looking at any of them, let them do what they liked with him, with his slave's disk, but made no answer. They grew more and more agitated and amazed at him, at this strange man who professed to be a Christian but who couldn't possibly be. His curious behaviour was beyond them. At last some of them went over to an old man who was sitting in the dark further inside the dungeon and who had not taken any part in what had been going on among them. After they had spoken to him for a while the old man got up and walked over with them to Barabbas.

He was a big man with a broad back who, despite a slight stoop, was still unusually tall. The powerful head had long but thinning hair, quite white, like his beard, which came right down over his chest. He had an imposing but very gentle expression; the blue eyes were almost childishly wide and clear though full of the wisdom of age.

He stood first looking for a long time at Barabbas, at his ravaged old face. Then he seemed to recollect something and nodded in confirmation.

—It's so long ago, he said apologetically, sitting down in the straw in front of him.

The others, who had gathered around, were very surprised. Did their greatly revered father know this man?

He evidently did, as they could see when he began talking to him. He asked him how he had got on during his life. And Barabbas told him what had happened to him. Not all, far from it, but enough for the other man to be able to understand or divine most of it. When he understood something Barabbas was unwilling to say, he merely nodded in silence. They had a good talk together, although it was so foreign to Barabbas to confide in anyone and though he didn't really do so now. But he answered the other's questions in a low, tired voice and even looked up now and again into the wise, childish eyes and at the furrowed old face, which was ravaged like his own but in quite a different way. The furrows were engraved deep into it, but it was all so different, and it radiated such peace. The skin in which they were engraved seemed almost white and the cheeks were hollow, probably because he had but few teeth left. But actually he had altered very little. And he still spoke his confident and ingenuous dialect.

The venerable old man gradually got to know both why the Lord's name was crossed out and why Barabbas had helped to set fire to Rome — that he had wanted to help them and their Saviour to set this world on fire. The old man shook his white head in distress when he heard this. He asked Barabbas how he could have thought it was they who had started the fire. It was Caesar himself who had had it done, the wild beast himself, and it was him Barabbas had helped.

— It was this worldly ruler you helped, he said, him to whom your slave's disk says you belong, not the Lord whose name is crossed out on it. Without knowing it, you served your rightful lord.

— Our Lord is Love, he added gently. And taking the disk that hung on Barabbas's chest amongst the grey hairs, he looked sorrowfully at his Lord and Master's crossed-out name.

He let it drop from his old fingers and sighed

heavily. For he realized that this was Barabbas's disk, the one he had to bear, and that there was nothing at all he could do to help him. And he realized that the other knew this too, saw it from his timid and solitary eyes.

— Who is he? Who is he? they all shouted when the old man got to his feet again. At first he didn't want to answer them, tried to get out of it. But they kept on at him until at last he was forced to do so.

— He is Barabbas, he who was acquitted in the Master's stead, he said.

They stared at the stranger, dumbfounded. Nothing could have astounded or upset them more than this.

— Barabbas! they whispered. Barabbas the acquitted! Barabbas the acquitted!

They didn't seem able to grasp it. And their eyes gleamed fierce and threatening in the semi-darkness.

But the old man quietened them.

— This is an unhappy man, he said, and we have no right to condemn him. We ourselves are full of faults and shortcomings, and it is no credit to us that the Lord has taken pity on us notwithstanding. We have no right to condemn a person because he has no god.

They stood with downcast eyes, and it was as

though they didn't dare to look at Barabbas after this, after these last terrible words. They moved away from him in silence to where they had been sitting before. The old man sighed and followed them with heavy steps.

Barabbas sat there again alone.

He sat there alone day after day in the prison, on one side, apart from them. He heard them sing their songs of faith and speak confidently of their death and the eternal life that awaited them. Especially after sentence had been pronounced did they speak of it a great deal. They were full of trust, there was not the slightest doubt amongst them.

Barabbas listened, deep in his own thoughts. He too thought of what was in store for him. He remembered the man on the Mount of Olives, the one who had shared his bread and salt with him and who was now long since dead again and lay grinning with his skull in the everlasting darkness.

Eternal life . . .

Was there any meaning in the life he had led? Not even that did he believe in. But this was something he knew nothing about. It was not for him to judge.

Over there sat the white-bearded old man among his own people, listening to them and talking to them

in his unmistakable Galilean dialect. But occasionally
he would lean his head in his big hand and sit there
for a moment in silence. Perhaps he was thinking of
the shore of Genesaret and that he would have liked
to die there. But it was not to be. He had met his
Master on the road and he had said: "Follow me."
And this he had had to do. He looked ahead of him
with his childlike eyes, and his furrowed face with
the hollow cheeks radiated a great peace.

And so they were led out to be crucified. They were
chained together in pairs, and, as they were not an
even number, Barabbas came last in the procession,
not chained to anyone. It just turned out like that.
In this way, too, it happened that he hung furthest out
in the rows of crosses.

A large crowd had collected, and it was a long time
before it was all over. But the crucified spoke consol-
ingly and hopefully to each other the whole time.
To Barabbas nobody spoke.

When dusk fell the spectators had already gone
home, tired of standing there any longer. And besides,
by that time the crucified were all dead.

Only Barabbas was left hanging there alone, still

alive. When he felt death approaching, that which he had always been so afraid of, he said out into the darkness, as though he were speaking to it:

— To thee I deliver up my soul.

And then he gave up the ghost.